Losing Independence

Tifani Clark

Losing Independence by Tifani Clark
© Tifani Clark 2016

Cover Design: Tifani Clark
Cover Image © via depositphotos.com
Photo ID: 6436425

ISBN-13: 978-0692677605
ISBN-10: 0692677607

An ABCD Publishing Book

http://www.tifaniclark.blogspot.com

Dedicated to those who never give up on their dreams.

Tifani Clark's
Holiday Novella Collection

One Night at Dornea Pines (Halloween - 2015)
All is Merri and Bright (Christmas - 2015)
A Little Bit of Luck (St. Patrick's Day - 2016)
Losing Independence (4th of July - 2016)

Other books by
Tifani Clark

Shadow of a Life
Haven Waiting
On Liberty's Watch

TABLE OF CONTENTS

Chapter 1

Lauren Walker grasped the zipper of her fiddle case and pulled it forward. The sound of the zipper moving around the case brought back memories of countless hours spent with her violin tucked under her chin, practicing until her fingers developed thick calluses. The smell of wood and rosin assailed her nose as she lifted the lid.

She pulled the instrument from its case and carefully plucked each string, listening with a trained ear for just the right tones. She turned each peg until the strings rang with the perfect pitch. Then, with a freshly rosined bow, she lifted her fiddle to her neck, placed the bow on the string, and closed her eyes. She took one deep breath and then opened her eyes, launching into a fiddling tune she'd practiced since her early teen years. It took that long to perfect it.

The tune started out slow and then picked up speed as she moved through the song, dipping and swaying her hips with the rhythm. Faster and faster her fingers flew as she played each note of the song in precise order. When the song ended, she tucked the fiddle under her arm and gave a dramatic bow.

Before she could rise from her position, her bedroom door burst open. Her roommate, Ashlyn, crossed the room and bounced onto Lauren's bed, blond curls spreading out on the pillows as she flopped back. "I see you're pretending you're on stage at the Grand Ole Opry again."

"And what's so wrong with that?" Lauren said with a wave of her violin's bow. "When I finally get my turn on that stage, I don't want to be embarrassed by not knowing how to bow properly."

Ashlyn laughed and sat up, tucking her legs under her petite frame. "I never said there was anything wrong with it. And trust me, when you make it to that stage, I'll be in the front row screaming for an encore. You can bow as much as you want and I'll keep clapping until they shut the lights off and lock the doors."

Lauren returned her bow to its case and sat on the bed next to Ashlyn as she gently wiped the rosin from the strings and wood of the violin. "Maybe we'll be on the stage together."

"Now *that* would be fun. We'd sing duets, then you'd fiddle while I sang a few solos." Ashlyn sighed and laid back against the pillows again. "Maybe we'd be accompanied by a cute drummer ..."

Lauren grinned. "Does the cute drummer in this story have a name?"

Ashlyn stared at the ceiling as she creased her eyebrows together, pretending to be deep in thought. "There's so many to choose from here in Nashville.

You know what I mean? I guess we could always ask Antoni. He knows his way around a drum set."

Lauren gently set her violin in its case and then tucked an emerald-colored blanket of velvet around it before zipping the case closed. She always felt as if she were tucking a child in at night when she put her violin away. In a way, she was. "You and Antoni have been dating for what ... two years?"

"Two years, one month, and twenty-three days ... but who's counting?"

"Okay, so you've been dating for quite a while," Lauren said. "Why is it we've never formed a band?"

"So little time, so much to do, maybe?" Ashlyn answered with a raise of her shoulders.

Lauren smiled. "Exactly. And speaking of little time, I need to get moving. My boss said she'll let me leave early tonight so I can get to my audition as long as I come in early." She looked down at her old gray sweatpants and t-shirt with a hole in the side. "I should probably shower."

"What are you trying to say? I feel like you're hinting at something."

Lauren picked up a pillow and threw it at Ashlyn's face. "It's not a hint. Get out of my room."

Ashlyn jumped up. "Yes, Ma'am," she said, saluting Lauren. "I need to get going anyway. I've got to get to work too."

"I thought it was your day off?"

"It is, but I'm filling in for Celeste who's 'sick' again." Ashlyn made air quotes with her fingers. "Antoni's picking me up from work and then we're going on our weekly dinner date so I'll be back late."

"Have fun, but not too much."

3

"Thanks. And good luck on your audition tonight," Ashlyn said just before shutting the bedroom door.

Lauren stood in the middle of her room, a frown covering her face. She'd been to countless auditions in the five years she'd lived in Nashville, but they never panned out. She didn't doubt her fiddling ability or her singing voice. She knew she had talent. Unfortunately, so did all the other aspiring musicians going to auditions and vying for open positions. Just once, she wanted someone to say, *"We like your sound. We want to hear more."* She wanted to hope that night's audition would be the one, but she doubted herself—something she'd been doing a lot lately.

She crossed the hall and took a quick shower before dressing in a button-up shirt, cowboy boots, and jeans—her usual work attire. She spent extra time curling her long brown locks and giving her hair plenty of volume. Her boss, Clarissa, insisted all the waitresses look as 'country' as possible when serving guests at Clarissa's Cowpoke Café. Lauren didn't mind the look, but knew her hair would lose much of its oomph after she covered it in a cowboy hat for her eight-hour shift.

She tossed a brush and hairspray into her bag along with extra makeup. She never went anywhere without her signature coral pink lipstick. With one last glance in the mirror, she grabbed her violin case and hurried out the door to her pickup. She'd driven the same rusty pickup since her high school days in Midway, Utah. It always took a little coaxing to get the engine going, but the truck had successfully seen her through five years of trying to make it big in Nashville.

"Come on, Betsy, don't fail me now," she

whispered as she pushed in the clutch and pumped the gas pedal. The engine sputtered and came to life. "I knew you wouldn't let me down. It's going to be a good day." She rubbed her hand on the dashboard and glanced at her violin case, tucked safely on the floor of the pickup's cab. "I have a feeling things are about to change for me."

Lauren shifted into first gear and then second as she pulled out of her parking spot on the road next to her apartment complex. The building wasn't fancy, but it was home—and the only thing she could afford on her wages and tips from the diner.

At Clarissa's Cowpoke Café, she parked her car in the back of the lot and placed her pink cowboy hat on her head, looking in the rearview mirror to make sure it was adjusted just right. She grabbed her fiddle case and bag and hurried through the back door of the restaurant. She didn't dare leave it in the truck while she worked.

A typical day in the back kitchen would be the cooks laughing and joking with the waitresses as they filled orders and called back and forth to each other. It was a noisy and boisterous place. That day, the mood was somber. No one laughed. Instead of shouting and chattering, everyone whispered. Each person turned and looked at Lauren as she entered. *Are those pity looks? Something's not right...*

Lauren grabbed the nearest waitress by the arm. "What's going on? Everyone looks ... sad."

The waitress shook her head and whispered, "We don't know what's going on. Clarissa posted a note next to the time clock. She said she's closing the restaurant early tonight and we're having a meeting with all employees."

Lauren's heart caught in her throat and she swallowed hard. "Did the note say why? She's never done anything like this before."

The waitress shook her head. "It didn't have any explanation. I have a bad feeling about it, though."

"I doubt it's anything good." Lauren clocked in, only briefly glancing at the note on the wall, and quickly tied a pink gingham apron around her waist before heading toward the restaurant floor. She didn't love her job, but she didn't hate it either. It paid the bills—barely—and gave her the chance to continue pursuing her music career in the city of her dreams.

"What can I get you this morning, Hank?" she asked the elderly gentleman sitting at a booth in the back corner of the diner.

He looked up and smiled, crinkles forming in the corners of his eyes. "How about my usual?"

"Coffee—black, no sugar, a double stack of pancakes with blueberry syrup, and two eggs over easy?"

"You know me well, Miss Lauren."

Lauren smiled. "I'll tell the kitchen to put a rush on it for my favorite customer." She stepped away from the table and on to her next. She had a lot of 'favorite customers.' It helped her tips go up. And honestly, she loved seeing the regulars come back and call her by name. It made them feel like family.

She only stopped for lunch and a couple short breaks during the day. By the time her shift ended—and the time of the dreaded meeting arrived—her feet throbbed. When the last customer exited and the only people left in the restaurant were employees, she tugged her boots off and climbed onto a barstool next to the counter. She rubbed her stockinged feet, hoping to ease some of the soreness before she had to stand for her audition. She glanced at her watch. *I hope this meeting doesn't take long. Being late for an audition is suicide in this town.*

"Thanks for those who are staying late and those who have come in on their day off," Clarissa began. "I know this meeting was planned on very short notice and I apologize for that." She stopped and cleared her throat, glancing at her husband standing next to her. "As many of you know, I've been running this diner for many years now. This week marks thirty years since we opened our doors. The first few years were rough and it took a while to get a faithful following, but we survived the lean years and became a thriving diner in a competitive world.

"I appreciate all of you who have worked with us for many years and those who are just becoming part of the Cowpoke family. You have given of yourselves and made this place better because of it." Clarissa paused and looked at each person in the room. "This last year has seen dwindling numbers as some of you have undoubtedly noticed. Two new restaurants have opened on this block in the past year and that's put a kink in our profits. The costs of operating the business versus the amount we make is rapidly narrowing. I'm getting old and the idea of fighting through another lean spell isn't exactly enticing. And so, it's with a heavy heart that I have decided to join my husband in retirement. After next week, Clarissa's Cowpoke Café will no longer be open."

Gasps could be heard throughout the room as each

employee took in the news. Lauren felt as if she'd been punched in the stomach. All the air seemed to drain from her as she fought to hold back the tears threatening to spill down her cheeks.

Clarissa continued her speech. "I know this is a shock and it puts all of you in unfortunate circumstances. Please know that I'm willing to write excellent letters of recommendation for any of you. We love all of you and wish the best for each of you wherever you end up."

Lauren finally gave up on trying to hold the tears back and let them fall. She was the first to throw her arms around Clarissa. The woman had been like a mother to her during the years she worked at the diner. She'd given Lauren—eighteen-years-old at the time—an opportunity and chance when no one else in Nashville did.

"You'll be okay, Lauren," Clarissa whispered as she wrapped her arms around her. "I know your turn is coming. You'll be so famous one day that all of this will seem like it never even happened. We'll be nothing but a blurb in your long biography."

Lauren laughed through her tears. "I hope you're right. I have an audition tonight. Maybe it's the one."

Clarissa unwound herself from Lauren's neck and squeezed her hands. "I'm sure it is. We'll be praying for you."

Lauren stepped back and let the other employees have a turn. They all loved the woman who treated them like her own children. She glanced down at her watch again. Only thirty-five minutes until her audition. The building wasn't far from the diner, but she wanted to have time to touch up her makeup—

especially since she'd been crying—and relax before her turn came. Hoping to prevent more tears, she avoided everyone else and slipped out the back door of the kitchen and into her truck.

That morning the audition had been an important goal. But now, in her new jobless state, the audition would be imperative to her survival. If she didn't have a steady income, she would have to leave Nashville—along with all her dreams.

Chapter 2

E very audition was the same for Lauren. She'd
find out about the event and get a tingle of
excitement starting in her heart and traveling
through her body, heightening all her senses. *This
could be my chance to break into the spotlight!* For
days beforehand, she'd walk with a little extra bounce
in her step. But, before the audition actually took
place, she'd convince herself it was hopeless—just
like all the other attempts—and persuade herself not
to even bother. She'd always realize her stupidity just
in time and sign up, knowing if she didn't try she'd
always wonder. The 'what ifs' kept her going through
years of disappointment.

That day she was auditioning to be a backup
singer with a country band called Tennessee Boots.
The band hadn't exactly hit it big yet, but their name
was starting to be recognized in some circuits. They'd
played many bars and venues around the city and the
south. Rumor had it they were on the verge of signing

a record deal.

Having auditioned in the building more than once, Lauren knew the restrooms were off to the right as soon as you entered. She kept her head down as she came through the front door and quickly stepped into the restroom to fix her hair and makeup before anyone took a good look at her.

She stared at her puffy eyes in the mirror and sighed. "Time to get to work," she mumbled to herself as she pulled out foundation, eyeliner, and eye shadow. She knew she only had a few minutes so she worked fast, ending her makeup job with a fresh coat of mascara.

Then, she bent over and flipped her brown hair upside down, finger combing it to add volume before standing up straight again and dousing it in hairspray. She stared at her pink cowboy hat and tapped her fingers on the edge of the sink. Sometimes she wore a hat for auditions and sometimes she didn't. Making a decision, she grabbed the hat and tucked it onto her head once more. Last, and most importantly in her mind, she trailed the tube of her favorite coral lipstick across her mouth and rubbed her lips together, making a kissing motion at herself in the mirror. "Knock their socks off," she whispered as she grinned at her image.

In the waiting room, only one person remained ahead of her. The meeting at the café had put a time restraint on her preparations. She set her violin case on the floor in a corner of the room and unzipped it. The bow received a run of the rosin on its hair and the strings a fresh tuning. Before she even stood up, her name was called at the door. She took one last deep breath and turned around, a smile plastered on her face. "Right here," she called.

Inside the audition room, three men she didn't recognize sat behind a table littered with papers— most likely the resumes of all the applicants. The entire Tennessee Boots band sat behind those men. Two of them played with their cell phones and two others whispered back and forth to each other. Her confidence level dropped a little. She rarely auditioned in front of the actual group. It could be a bad thing or a good thing. With how bored they looked before she even began, chances of impressing them weren't good.

"State your name," the gentleman on the right said as he pushed his glasses up the bridge of his nose.

"I'm Lauren Walker and I'm a country girl from way out west," she said, continuing to smile despite her pounding heart.

The men gave no reaction and the band members continued to do what they'd been doing when she first walked in.

"I see you've brought a violin. Were you not aware this was a singing audition?" the same man asked.

"Yes," Lauren said. "I plan to sing an original song. I brought this along in case you wanted to see my diversity."

"We already have a fiddle player in the band," the man said with a wave of his hand.

Lauren tried not to let the man's brusqueness get to her. "Well then, I'll just have to let my voice leave the good impressions."

"We'll be recording this audition tonight. Is that okay with you?"

Lauren nodded once. "That's fine."

"Very well. Please begin when you're ready."

Truth be told, Lauren took her violin to every audition whether it was for a voice audition or a musician audition. She thought of it as her safety blanket. If she clutched it, her fingers were less likely to tremble.

With all the confidence she could muster, Lauren stepped closer to the microphone in the middle of the room and closed her eyes. She took a deep breath and then opened her eyes as she began to sing. The song she chose had special meaning to her. It told the story of a girl setting out on her own, finding her own independence as she chased her dreams. She wrote it during her first year in Nashville ... and it told *her* story.

Lauren sang her heart out, ending with a long held note that filled the room with a gentle, soothing sound before drifting off. Lauren took a step back from the microphone and nodded to the judges. She dared to glance at the band. Two of the members were no longer preoccupied and one even sat on the edge of his seat—a good sign.

"Thank you, that will be all," the gentleman on the right said without looking up.

"Would you like to hear any fiddling before I leave?" Lauren asked boldly.

"No thanks. This is the last night of auditions. If you don't hear from us by midnight, the answer's no." He shuffled the papers on the table, still not looking up.

"Thank you for this opportunity," Lauren said as she left the room. She forced the smile to stay on her face even though her confidence waned. Just before the door shut behind her, she saw the same band member who appeared interested only moments before give her a nod of the head and a smile. *He liked it. Please, oh please, let him have some influence on the others in that room tonight.*

Back in the waiting room, Lauren glanced around. Three others were lined up and waiting for their turn to audition. She recognized two of them from other auditions she'd been to. They'd be tough competition.

She carefully zipped her violin back in its case and slipped out of the building. *What happened to that feeling you had this morning that today was your day? Something better start changing ... fast.*

Once inside Betsy, she lowered her head to the steering wheel and let the worries of the evening wash out. First thing in the morning, if she didn't hear from Tennessee Boots, she'd scour the area for job openings and more auditions. Living paycheck to paycheck made finding a new source of income her main priority.

Inside her purse, the cell phone she'd muted during her audition vibrated. She dug through the purse's contents until she felt the familiar texture of her phone case. "Hello?"

"*Hey, have you auditioned yet?*" Brendan asked.

She smiled at the calming sound of her boyfriend's voice. "I just finished. I'm sitting in my truck outside the building trying to generate enough energy to drive home."

"*Those things always drain you.*"

Lauren twisted a lock of hair around her finger. "I have a lot riding on them."

Brendan cleared his throat. *"Have you eaten dinner yet?"*

"Not yet. I haven't had the best day."

He paused. *"I'm sorry. How about we meet up for dinner? Somewhere nice."* He cleared his throat again. It wasn't like him.

"Are you getting a cold?"

"I feel fine. There's just something I wanted to talk to you about."

"I'd like that. After the day I've had, I could use a good dinner. Where should I meet you?"

"How about Abbott's?"

Lauren's eyebrows shot up. "Seriously?"

"Why not?"

"It's ... expensive."

"We've always said we'd go there sometime. Why not tonight?"

Lauren had been dating Brendan for almost four years. They met at an audition shortly after she arrived in Nashville and became fast friends. Brendan ran the technical, behind-the-scenes stuff like lights and sound equipment. Eight months later, they started dating. The idea of marriage had come up before, but they both agreed it would be best to wait until they had their feet planted solidly in one way or another.

Lauren's mind raced. *Is tonight the night? Is he going to propose? Maybe that's why I had a good feeling about today. Losing my job was horrible, the audition didn't go as I wanted, but ... maybe there's still hope for the day.*

"Are you still there?" Brendan asked.

"Yes, I'm here." Lauren shook her head to clear her

mind. "I'm just leaving the parking lot. I'll meet you at Abbott's in fifteen minutes."

"*Perfect.*"

Lauren's nerves threatened to get the better of her as she drove across town. Her marriage proposal was something she'd dreamed of her entire life. She'd never wanted a showy display of affection or a grandiose attempt to make the proposer look better— like proposing on a jumbotron at a ball game or concert. No. She wanted something intimate. Something sweet. Something ... like a quiet dinner at Abbott's. Brendan knew that about her. She'd mentioned it more than once.

Heart racing, she tucked a jacket around her violin case to keep it hidden from the view of passersby and stepped out of rusty Betsy. She started to shut the door of the pickup but remembered she still wore her hat and tossed it inside on the seat. She finger combed her hair again, wondering if she still looked okay. If a proposal came with the dinner, she'd insist on their waitress taking a photo of them to commemorate the event. She didn't want the stress of the day showing in the picture.

Brendan stood near the front door, hands stuffed down in his pockets. He paced back and forth. *He's nervous. He's never nervous. This is really going to happen.*

"You look great," Brendan said, as he pulled a hand from his pocket and took her hand. He leaned forward and gave her a quick kiss.

In her cowboy boots, Lauren stood as tall as Brendan. "I probably look like I just worked an eight-hour-shift on my feet, but thanks. And you don't look so bad yourself. Is this a new shirt?"

Brendan glanced down and a hint of color reddened his cheeks. "Does it look okay?"

"I like it. It brings out the blue in those eyes of yours I love so much," Lauren said as she leaned into him, putting a hand on his chest.

Brendan's cheek color deepened and he stepped back. "Let's go inside. I called in a reservation for us. I'm sure our table's ready by now."

He took her hand and pulled her to the front door. Lauren had a brief moment of panic when she considered the fact that she wore jeans to a fancy restaurant, but then remembered what town she was in and pushed the thought from her mind.

"So, how was your day?" Brendan asked when they were seated at a corner booth. "You mentioned on the phone that it hadn't been the best."

Lauren leaned forward in her chair to smell the fresh roses in a vase next to a flickering candle. *Do I tell him the truth or wait until after he proposes so I don't spoil our evening?* "Just a tough day at work. Nothing I can't bounce back from," she finally answered. *I hope.*

Brendan folded his hands on top of the menu. "That's good. And the audition?"

"If I don't hear from them by midnight, I didn't get the job."

"That's all you have to say?" Brendan smiled. "Did you sing *and* play?"

"I only sang. They didn't want to hear me play."

Brendan nodded slowly.

Lauren frowned. "I know, I know. Not a good sign."

"Not necessarily. Maybe your singing impressed

17

them so much, they didn't need to hear anything else."

"I did manage to pull two of the band members' attentions away from their phones long enough to acknowledge my performance," she said, sitting up straighter.

"See? Way to see the positive in it."

The waiter arrived to take their orders. Brendan insisted she order whatever she wanted, furthering her assumption that her day had finally taken a turn for the better. She ordered lobster ravioli with a green salad on the side.

Brendan ordered a steak, exactly like she knew he would. They'd been together so long, she could predict his behavior and responses in almost everything he did. She pictured how it would be when they were together permanently and smiled. They made a good pair.

Lauren only had a few bites of dinner left when Brendan cleared his throat and looked at her with a facial expression she'd never seen before. It seemed to be a cross between nervousness, fear, and fondness. She carefully set her fork down and dabbed at the edges of her mouth with her cloth napkin.

"There's ... umm ... something I wanted to talk to you about tonight," Brendan began. He stuffed his hand in his pocket and then pulled it out again, keeping it hidden under the table.

Lauren couldn't peel her eyes away from his arm. Any moment he'd be revealing a ring box. Her heart raced. "Yes?"

"We've been together for a long time, right?"

"A very long time."

"And it's been nice, right?"

"Some of the best years of my life." Lauren smiled and reached for his free hand across the table.

Brendan caught her eyes and then quickly looked down at their clasped hands. "I agree. That's why it hurts me to do what I'm about to do."

Lauren's smile faltered. "It ... *hurts* you?"

Brendan continued to stare at the table, but he pulled his hand away from hers. "Do you remember meeting Jennifer, the girl I went to high school with, a few weeks ago?"

Lauren couldn't imagine where the conversation was headed. "Is that the girl we bumped into at the grocery store?"

"Uh huh." Brendan nodded. "I may have been a little vague at the time, but Jennifer and I dated in high school—for two years. We broke up after graduation. She was going to college and I was coming here. Anyway, after you and I bumped into her a few weeks ago, she contacted me." He stopped and took a deep breath. "Jennifer and I have decided to get back together and give our relationship another shot."

Lauren felt like she'd been punched in the stomach for the second time that day. The meal she'd just finished threatened to make another appearance. She reached for her water glass and took little sips, willing her dinner to stay put.

"I never wanted to hurt you. I honestly care about you. Never in a million years did I expect this to happen. It's just ... well ... Jennifer and I have a history together and we're from the same hometown. It makes sense. We've got to give it another shot." Brendan leaned across the table. "Say something, Lauren. I'm floundering here."

Lauren looked up at him with tear-filled eyes. "What do you want me to say?" she whispered.

"Tell me you won't hate me. Tell me it's okay and you'll move on and you were secretly thinking of breaking up with me anyway," he pleaded.

Lauren shook her head. "I could say those things, but they'd all be lies."

Brendan folded his arms over his chest and looked away. "I really didn't want to hurt you. You're one of my best friends. I care about you. Can you forgive me?"

With trembling fingers and carefully calculated breathing, Lauren reached for her purse on the chair next to her. "I can't make any promises. See ya around."

She stood and walked away from the table as quickly as she could, hoping to get away before he followed her—*if* he tried to follow her. She kept her head held high as she passed other customers and wait staff. A few shot her looks, but thankfully their eyes didn't linger. If they did, they might have noticed the silent tears sliding down her cheeks as she pushed her way through the doors and into the parking lot.

Chapter 3

L auren didn't immediately drive back to her apartment. Instead, she drove the streets of Nashville, looking into store windows and watching tourists and residents as they went about their evening. They all appeared to have a purpose, a reason for living and being. In one day's time, all of her purpose had been taken from her.

She tried to convince herself that Brendan wasn't worth a broken heart, but she couldn't do it. He'd been part of her long-term goals for years, and now those goals lay shattered on the floor of Abbott's Restaurant.

"I should have ordered an expensive dessert, too," she mumbled to herself before pulling into the parking lot of a grocery store. She wiped at her eyes before opening her creaky truck door. She brought her pink cowboy hat along so she could tuck it down low over her face, covering up her red-rimmed blue eyes.

Once inside, she headed straight for the frozen food section and the chocolate ice cream. She reached for her favorite kind, but then stopped herself. Her favorite kind—with chunks of brownie and caramel swirls—happened to be one of the most expensive brands on the shelves. She had no job and no boyfriend. The little money she had would need to stretch farther than ever. With a sigh, she chose a pint of a different, cheaper brand and headed for the front of the store to pay for it.

Ashlyn was still on her date when Lauren got home, a fact that brought some relief. Alone in her dark bedroom, Lauren pulled the lid from the ice cream and dug into it with a soup spoon she'd grabbed from a kitchen drawer on her way through the apartment. She spooned the creamy dessert into her mouth, one giant bite after another, until the contents were completely gone. Then, she lay on her bed and let the tears flow.

She cried like she'd never cried before. She cried for the pain, the fear, the loss, the regrets, and the unknown. When she couldn't coax any more tears from her swollen eyes, she sat up and threw the empty ice cream tub in the wastebasket. She splashed cold water on her face inside the bathroom before returning to her room and stripping out of her clothes. The sweatpants and old t-shirt she'd been wearing earlier that day still sat on the edge of her bed and she pulled them on again.

Since her arrival home, she'd avoided looking at the clock, but now she sat on her bed with her eyes glued to the red glow of the alarm clock. The minutes ticked by, getting closer and closer to midnight. Until she saw that magical number on the clock, her dreams still had a chance of coming true.

Eleven eighteen. Eleven twenty-two. Eleven thirty-seven. She checked her phone, reassuring herself that it did indeed have enough battery life to accept a call. Eleven forty-three. Eleven forty-nine. Eleven fifty-six.

Midnight.

Her cell remained silent.

"That's it. I'm done." She picked up her phone and threw it across the room. It bounced off her dresser and landed in the pile of clothes she'd just taken off. "I didn't want to sing with your stupid band anyway," she muttered.

The sound of the apartment door opening and closing startled her and she slid under the covers on her bed, pulling them up around her chin. The familiar sound of the deadbolt and lock being clicked into place and the sound of Ashlyn's footsteps across their fake hardwood floors temporarily kept her mind occupied. Usually Ashlyn came in quietly, showered, and slipped into her own room without waking Lauren up. Their sleep schedules had never been the same.

That night, a soft tap sounded on Lauren's door. "Lauren? Are you still awake?" Ashlyn's voice carried through the door.

Lauren cleared her throat. "Sort of," she called back.

"Can I come in?"

No. "Yes."

Ashlyn threw the door open and bounded into the room. She had more energy at all times than anyone else Lauren knew. Much to Lauren's dismay, Ashlyn reached for the light switch and flipped it on. "Whoa," Ashlyn said, taking a step back. "You look like crap." She also had the least tact.

Lauren squinted in the bright light. "I always look like crap this time of night. And it was a rough day." *I don't have enough energy to tell her my sob story tonight. It can wait until morning.*

"I'm sorry. How'd your audition go?"

"That was part of the bad day," Lauren mumbled.

Ashlyn frowned, but mercifully dropped the subject. "So, Antoni and I went out tonight."

Lauren pressed the palms of her hands into her eyes. "You mentioned you were going to do that."

"We had a nice dinner."

"I'm glad." *Now please leave so I can get some sleep.*

"Lauren, you won't even look at me."

Lauren pulled her hands away from her face and looked at her friend.

Ashlyn stuck her hand out, palm down. "We're engaged!"

Another punch to the stomach. "You're ... engaged?"

Ashlyn's head bobbed up and down. "Uh huh. He asked me at the restaurant. The waitress was in on it and everything. It was so sweet and so romantic. I can't believe it happened."

Lauren swallowed hard. "I'm so happy for you."

Ashlyn didn't notice the strain in Lauren's voice and continued her tale. "Neither of us is interested in a big, fancy wedding. They take too much time and effort to plan. We talked about it and we're going to elope. Can you believe that?"

Lauren opened her mouth, but Ashlyn didn't wait

for a response.

"Antoni's parents have a condo on the beach in Maui. We're going to get married there with just our parents as witnesses, and then we'll honeymoon in Hawaii." She grabbed Lauren's hands. "Can you believe this is happening?"

Shoot me now. "It's exciting."

Ashlyn threw her head back and laughed. "I can tell you're tired. You don't function well this late. We'll talk more in the morning, okay?" She stood and crossed the room to the door, turning off the light. "Oh, and since Antoni and I plan on doing this really soon, you might want to place an ad for a new roommate sooner rather than later. I'd feel bad if you had to pay both halves of the rent for very long. Love ya!"

Ashlyn shut the door and Lauren lay back against her pillows, bracing herself for a second round of open floodgates.

Lauren tried, but she couldn't sleep. She tossed and turned, sat up, and laid back down. Over and over. Her mind replayed the scenarios of the previous day on a repeating reel. She pictured herself going to work and finding out about the meeting. Clarissa's face as she told everyone about the store's closing wouldn't leave her mind. Then, she watched herself, as if from behind a sheer curtain, as she sang her heart out for a band where only two members bothered to look up. The minutes ticked by on the clock in her head and she relived the moment midnight came and she knew she didn't get the job. Next, the scene in Abbott's restaurant would replay. She'd never gone from pure joy to heartbreak as fast as she did while sitting in the chair, smelling roses, and watching the man she thought she loved in the flickering candlelight.

And finally, she relived the memory of Ashlyn proclaiming that all her dreams were coming true. Lauren was happy for her, she couldn't deny that, but the happiness came with a huge serving of jealousy.

Hopes and dreams were scattered everywhere and try as she might, she couldn't think of a way to gather them back up. It reminded her of the time she and a group of friends entered the contest to catch a greased pig at the county fair in elementary school. Each time she thought she had a grip on the pig, it would slip out of her hands and leave her face first in the mud.

What am I going to do for money? Who am I going to get to live here with me? If my heart ever heals, when will I find time to fall in love again? I'm going to have to work two jobs. If I'm working two jobs, how can I go to any more auditions? If I don't continue to audition, what's the point of being here?

Giving up on ever finding sleep, she crawled from her bed for the last time that night and sat at her little desk in the corner of the room. She turned on the lamp. It was one of the few items she'd brought with her when she left Midway, Utah. A plaster cowboy with his hat tucked over his face and a piece of straw hanging from his mouth lounged against the post of the lamp, painted to look like a tree trunk. The green lampshade itself dropped down over the sides as if it were the leaves of the tree.

"Wake up and tell me what to do, Henry," she

whispered to the figurine. Not surprisingly, the lamp didn't respond.

Lauren pulled a piece of paper and a pencil from the drawer of the desk and drew a line straight down the middle. On one side she wrote *Pros* and on the other side she wrote *Cons*. After lying awake the entire night, she could only think of one solution to her problem, a solution that made her heart race and her stomach churn. She had to find another way. With head bent, she began to write, her pencil scratching against the paper as she hurried to get everything down. When she finished, she leaned back in her chair and looked at the results of her efforts.

Anyone not close to the situation would take one look at the paper and assume the decision was an easy one to make. One side of the paper was filled from top to bottom. The other side held only a few words.

Lauren rose from the desk and peeked out the blinds of her bedroom window. The sun had already risen and the world was once again coming alive. She couldn't put it off any longer. With a deep sigh of resignation, she crossed the room and picked up her cell phone from the pile of clothes she'd tossed it onto the night before. A chip in the corner of the case marked where it hit the dresser in her moment of rage. *One more thing on my list of things gone wrong.*

She sat on the edge of her bed and turned the phone on. The time difference might be a problem, but if she waited any longer, she would chicken out. With a determined effort, she punched in the phone number she knew by heart.

One ring. Two rings. Three rings.

"*Hello?*"

"Mom? It's Lauren." She swallowed to keep her voice steady. "I'm coming home."

Chapter 4

The screen door of the familiar farmhouse opened and closed as Lauren's dad turned onto the gravel driveway, and a figure stepped out onto the porch. Lauren's mom must have been watching from the kitchen window. It offered the best view of the long lane leading to the house.

Her dad parked his truck in front of the garage. Lauren couldn't remember him ever parking inside. Instead, the garage overflowed with hobbies, tools, and long forgotten junk.

She longed to park Betsy in front of that garage again. Losing her truck had been the final slap in her face as she left Nashville. After packing its bed with all the belongings she couldn't—or didn't want to—sell, she set off on the long drive across the country. Just before she crossed from Colorado into Utah, Betsy's engine blew. Despite her pleas to the truck, it wouldn't run. She used every last cent she had to get it towed to a mechanic's shop only to be told the cost of repairs would be more than the truck's value, which wasn't a lot. Once again, she swallowed her pride and called home. Her dad drove to Colorado and picked her up.

She reached for the door handle, but her dad stretched out his hand and rested it on her shoulder. "It'll be nice to have you home. We've really missed you around here," he said.

Lauren patted his hand on her shoulder. "Thanks, Daddy. I've missed you and this place, too." *And that's only a partial lie.* She stepped from the truck and closed her eyes, taking a deep breath and filling her lungs with the familiar mountain air. Five years since she'd been home, but the smell brought memories of her early years flooding back.

"Don't just stand there!" a woman's voice called. "Get over here and give me a hug!"

Lauren opened her eyes and grinned at her mom. She stood on the porch with her hands on her hips. Dressed in jeans and an old t-shirt, her mom looked exactly the same as she did the day Lauren drove away.

"It's good to see you, Lulu," she said as her mother's arms came around her. Everyone called her mom Lulu, and that included all four of her children. Lauren didn't know where the nickname came from and didn't think her mom even knew. It was just the name she'd always gone by.

"It better be good to see me. Five long years away and the only time we got to see you were the two times your dad and I flew out to Tennessee. That's just not right." She winked.

Lauren shrugged as she ran her hand over her

mother's hair. When she left Midway, more blond peeked through the gray, now the opposite was true. "Airline tickets are expensive and lowly waitresses don't have any paid vacation time."

Lulu shook her head and grabbed Lauren's hand, pulling her into the house while her dad retrieved the luggage from the back of his pickup. "It doesn't matter now. All water under the bridge as they say. What's important is that you're back and you can get on with life."

Lauren bit her lip. When she made the decision to return to Midway, she did it with the intent to get a job and live with her parents until she had enough money to return to Nashville. She was one of only a few people in her graduating class who managed to get away from their quaint lives in the little town. She didn't want to get pulled back in unless she knew there would be a way back out. "It's just temporary, Mom."

Lulu waved her hand. "That's what you think. I intend to fill you so full of good home cooking and love that you'll never want to leave again."

"Good luck with that." Lauren didn't bother to mention that she'd lived in a land of southern home cooking for the past five years.

Lauren's dad held up her violin case. "Where do you want this?"

In her tiny Nashville apartment she kept it in her bedroom at all times. The farmhouse had more space. "Just set it by the piano."

Her dad gently set it on the floor. "Aww ... it looks so good back in its usual spot. I can't tell you how much I've missed the sound of that thing around here." He straightened and picked up the rest of her bags he'd set by the front door. "Want me to carry these upstairs for you?"

"I can get them. Thanks, Daddy."

"No problem. I'll be over at the cabins. If anyone needs me, just radio over." He tipped his hat to Lauren and Lulu and pushed the screen door open.

Lauren lifted a bag to her shoulder and carried one in each hand. "I assume I'm back in my old bedroom?"

"Of course," Lulu said. "It's where you belong." She pulled one of the bags off Lauren's shoulder and hurried up the stairs to the first door on the right. "We didn't change anything. Kept it just like you left it."

Lauren slowly pushed on the door to her old bedroom. As promised, the room looked the way it had when she left five years before. Posters of singers and bands filled her walls. Some of the bands weren't together anymore and some had grown even more famous. She smiled as she spotted a couple band members she met in person while in Nashville.

The top of her white dresser still held a row of trophies and medals she'd won at fiddling competitions and talent shows all over the state. Each had a thick layer of dust.

"You didn't have to keep all this stuff out, you know." Lauren picked up an old textbook sitting on the bookshelf and examined it. "I'm pretty sure I was supposed to return this to the high school," she mumbled. "I wonder what the late fee would be for something that's five years overdue."

Lulu sat on the edge of the twin-sized bed. "Why would I pack up your stuff? What if I got rid of something you wanted to keep? I thought about dusting, but things have been a little crazy around here and I never got the chance."

"Most of this stuff is junk. I'll never use it again."

"You might say that now, but years from now, when you're my age, you might wish you kept some of this *stuff* for memory's sake."

"That's doubtful." Lauren set the textbook down and turned toward the bed. She cringed at the sight of the frilly pink bedspread with little white flowers embroidered around the edge. It looked like something from a ten-year-old girl's room. In fact, she was pretty sure that's how old she was when her parents gave her the bedding for Christmas.

"I wish I'd had room to bring more stuff back from Tennessee. My blankets were in better condition. And the color was better."

"What's wrong with this?" Lauren's mom ran her hands across the bedspread. "You used to love this."

"Exactly. I *used* to love it. I'm an adult now."

Lulu sighed. "I know, but you'll always be my little girl. That's what happens when you're the youngest child."

"Speaking of children, how are my favorite brothers?"

Lulu grinned. Talking about her kids and grandkids was her favorite pastime. "They're all doing great. John and Michelle moved into their new house two years ago now, but you haven't seen it yet, obviously. There's plenty of room for their kids to run around. You'll be impressed with it."

"John sent pictures every year. I can't believe how big the boys are. They probably won't remember me even though I used to babysit them all the time when they were babies." Lauren picked up a framed photo on her nightstand and frowned when she saw who was in it with her. She set it back in place—face down.

"We see them every month or two. If they don't come here, we drive to their house. The kids will get to know you again. They're friendly."

"What about Nathan?" Lauren asked.

"Same old, same old. He's still working at the same computer store. He loves it and has no intention of ever leaving."

Lauren turned to Lulu. "If he makes good money, and he loves it, why leave?"

Lulu pursed her lips together. "That's true."

"Any prospects in the marriage department yet?"

"He doesn't stop working long enough to go on a single date, let alone have an actual relationship. Maybe now that you're back you can convince him to get on with that."

Lauren stopped examining her room and sat on the bed next to her mom. "I'll do my best. And Shane and Amanda? I've never met their baby."

A giant grin spread across Lulu's face. "He's not much of a baby anymore. Toddler would be a more appropriate word." She cleared her throat. "They have some exciting news they were going to call you about, but when they found out you were coming back home they decided to wait until you got here to tell you."

Lauren raised her eyebrows. "What kind of news?"

"I promised I wouldn't tell." Lulu chewed on her lip, a habit Lauren got from her.

"Is Amanda pregnant again?"

Lulu picked at one of the white flowers on the

bedspread. "Maybe."

Lauren stared at her mom's face. She could always get her to crack. "Is she having a girl? Are you finally going to have a granddaughter?"

Lulu didn't respond, but the look on her face filled in the silence.

"I knew it! I'm so excited for them. We girls are outnumbered in the Walker family. It's about time we have an increase in our numbers."

"Lauren, do *not* let them know I told you. They really wanted it to be a surprise," Lulu said, pleading with her eyes.

"If they wanted it to be a surprise, why did they tell you? You've never been good at keeping secrets. Everyone knows that."

Lulu opened her mouth as if to protest, but then shut it again. "You're right. Bad choice on their part. Just try to act surprised."

"Cross my heart and hope to die."

Lulu slapped her hands on her thighs and stood up. "I better get back to the kitchen. We've got big numbers for tonight's dinner. I need to get cracking on the bread dough."

Lauren grabbed Lulu's arm before she could slip through the door. "Tonight's dinner? You didn't tell me you invited guests for my first night back. You couldn't give me one night to settle?"

Lulu's eyes shifted to the hallway staircase and then to the ceiling, looking everywhere but at Lauren. "Your dad and I have been meaning to tell you about something. It just never felt like the right time."

"Mom?"

"We didn't want to upset you."

"I'm getting upset because you won't tell me what's going on." Lauren's voice rose in pitch a few notes. "If it's something you purposely kept from me, I'm probably not going to like it no matter how long you hide it so you might as well get it over with. Spill it."

"It's not that big of a deal, really. We still have the cabins to rent out, but last fall we were approached about another business opportunity and decided to take it."

Lauren raised her eyebrows. If there was one thing about her parents she knew, it was that they valued consistency. They dressed the same as they had their entire lives, they ate the same foods, visited the same places, and had the same job.

Set against the majestic Wasatch mountains, Midway offered spectacular views of their alpine farmhouse. It's proximity to Park City and world-class skiing brought visitors from all over to the area. Her parents owned a 'hotel' that consisted of thirty tiny cabins. Each contained one or two beds, a small bathroom, and a little kitchenette. Guests filled them at all times of the year.

Lulu glanced at the stairs again. "Follow me to the kitchen and I'll explain everything."

Lauren trailed behind her mom, apprehension growing with each step. She climbed onto a barstool and leaned on her elbows as her mom kneaded and rolled a huge ball of bread dough. "That's enough to feed a small army. Why are you making so much?"

"That's part of the story." Lulu glanced at Lauren and then focused on the dough again. "At the beginning of the year, one of the local ranchers approached us about joining forces to promote both our businesses. He wanted to turn part of his ranch into a dude ranch of sorts. He's offering riding lessons, guided hikes, square dancing, roping, everything you'd expect at that kind of a place. He also wanted to have a nightly dinner show where locals and tourists alike can come and get a feel for the old west."

"Where do you and Daddy fit into all this?"

"His one hang up was not having the resources yet to build a bunkhouse for his guests. Dad and I agreed to combine Walker Cabin Rentals with his ranch and to help with the nightly dinner show in exchange for a percentage of the profits. This is the first summer, but we've had sold out crowds almost every day. So far, the dinners have just been previews—test runs if you will—with a few chosen locals and cabin guests. The official opening will be on the 4th of July."

Lauren's eyes widened. "Lulu, this is wonderful news! Progress is *not* a bad thing. Why didn't you want me to know about it? I'm excited for you."

Lulu returned her attention to the bread dough, pounding her fist into the ball with more vigor than before. "Because," she said quietly. "I didn't know how you'd feel about our partner."

Fear pricked at the back of Lauren's consciousness. "Who is it?"

"The dude ranch is the Double Wind Ranch. We're now partners with Scott McCallister."

Chapter 5

Lauren swallowed hard and took a moment to collect her thoughts before calmly answering. "You can do business with Scott. It has nothing to do with me."

Lulu reached over and took her hand, leaving a puff of flour on Lauren's palm. "I know, sweetie, but ... it's just that you left here on such poor terms with him. I don't want you to take off again because of this."

Lauren bit her lip, attempting to keep her cool. "Scott is *not* the reason I left Midway. We're both adults now. Anything bad that happened between us is so far in the past, it doesn't matter anymore. I doubt he even remembers."

Lulu blew her breath out. "You can't begin to imagine how relieved I am to hear that. I've been worrying about telling you ever since you called to say you were coming home."

"Worry no more. I'm fine," she lied, stuffing a trembling hand in her pocket. "I'm sure Scott and I will see each other at some point. It might be nice to have a conversation starter so it's not as awkward. I'll have him tell me about the new business."

"Way to be positive, hon."

Lauren climbed off the barstool and looked out the kitchen window. Her dad's truck was no longer parked in front of the garage. "Do you think Daddy would mind if I took the four-wheeler? I want to go over and see the cabins. After all, it's been five years since I've been here. They're as much a part of home as this house."

Lulu frowned and wiped a hand across her face, leaving a trail of flour behind. "We don't have the four-wheeler anymore. Dad replaced it with a couple golf carts."

Lauren started to laugh, but then noted Lulu's serious expression. "You're not kidding. He golfs now? That's something I want to see."

"Heavens no," Lulu said with a wave of her hand. "That will never happen. It's just easier to transport guests who don't want to walk from the cabins to the Double Wind on a golf cart than it is on a four wheeler. One of the carts has two rows."

"So ... can I take a golf cart?"

"They're both at the cabins."

"Oh." Lauren slumped back onto the barstool. She felt trapped, something she hadn't experienced since she left Midway five years before. Losing her independence chafed. Walking to the cabins was a possibility, but it would be an almost two mile walk on a gravel road under a hot summer sun. Her mom had never had a car of her own. Lauren's parents were so inseparable, they didn't see the point in getting something else. If one of them went somewhere away from home, they both went.

While Lauren watched, Lulu expertly shaped the dough into eight loaves and set each in a cloth-covered pan under the kitchen window. "After the grand opening, I'll have to make more bread each day. Right now, we're keeping the numbers small."

"What else do you plan on serving?" Lauren asked.

"Scott has a ranch hand that makes barbecue chicken and baked beans each day. Add a thick slice of fresh bread and butter and it's a good meal."

"No dessert?" Lauren joked.

Lulu waved a wooden spoon at her. "Actually, we finally found a use for the raspberry bushes that grow out of control behind the house. Dessert is a scoop of vanilla ice cream with raspberry topping. Instead of cutting the bushes back this year, we planted more."

"My mouth is watering just thinking about it. I might have to come for dinner one of these nights."

"Of course. You're always invited." Lulu turned her attention to the dishes in the sink. "Your dad and I wanted to offer you a job cleaning the cabins this summer. You already know the ropes. I know it's not what you want, but we could use the help with the extra work we now have and unless I'm wrong, you could use the money."

Lauren grew up cleaning the cabins when guests checked out. All her spending money came from that place. She thought she'd moved on from it. "I hope to find a job in town somewhere, but I can work for you until then."

Lulu smiled. "Good. I'll let your dad know. You can start in the morning. Every cabin is booked tomorrow night so it will be a busy morning getting things ready." She stopped working and turned to Lauren. "I think your old bicycle is still in the garage, you know, if you want to go over there this afternoon."

"I haven't ridden a bike since I was a kid. I doubt I remember how."

"No one forgets how to ride a bike."

Lauren sighed and stood up again. "Maybe I'll give it a shot. I'll be back in a couple hours."

She walked to the garage and lifted the rolling door, revealing a space stuffed with more random objects than any one family should ever accumulate. It took a little digging, and a few knocked over boxes, but she managed to extricate the bicycle from the mess. With two flat tires, she wouldn't be going anywhere. Once again, she ventured into the garage and shoved things aside until she found her dad's air compressor. The bike tires filled with air and, much to her relief, held their shape.

She shut the garage door and balanced on the seat of the bike. "Here goes nothing," she muttered as she pushed off with one foot. The first few rotations of the wheels were shaky, but she soon got into the groove. Lulu was right: no one forgets how to ride a bike.

Even though the hot sun caused sweat to drip down her back and forehead, she found the activity energizing. It lightened her mood and she found herself enjoying the ride through the countryside. The only thing that would have made it better was if the bike wasn't pink with a silver basket strapped to the front. The bike had been exactly what she wanted—when she was twelve.

Walker Cabin Rentals lay on the border of the

Double Wind Ranch. The ranch curved around her parents' property, touching borders on three sides. The part of the ranch closest to the cabins held barns and sheds. Lauren imagined that was where the dude ranch would be. The actual McAllister home sat on the opposite side of the ranch, a five minute walk from the Walker farmhouse. Growing up, Scott and Lauren had been best friends. Being the same age, and living on the outskirts of a small town, they didn't have much choice in that department.

The pair did everything together: swimming in the reservoir, riding Scott's horses, fly fishing on the river, or chasing each other around the cabin rentals. They both had other friends—including boyfriends and girlfriends—but always stuck together.

Until Lauren left for Nashville.

She left for Tennessee only a few days after graduation. It was something she'd talked about doing her entire life, but those closest to her assumed the dream would eventually die, never really believing she'd go through with it. Her parents tried to convince her to stay, but they didn't succeed. At eighteen, she could legally do what she wanted.

A bump and a pop pulled her thoughts from her hometown and back to the road in front of her. The front wheel of the bike was quickly losing its air and she could barely turn the pedals on the gravel road. She climbed off the bike seat and inspected the wheel. Two thorns pierced the rubber, leaving no hope for an easy fix.

"Seriously?" she yelled as she shoved the bike to the edge of the road. "I can't take any more of this! My job, my boyfriend, my music career, my truck, and now this!" She closed her eyes and screamed, letting the frustrations of the previous two weeks rush out of her. Her voice echoed through the low-lying hills and came back to her. Instead of crying, she sat down in the gravel and laughed—until she cried. Fate could do what it wanted—she was giving up.

She wasn't sure how long she sat on the side of the road, but she lifted her head from her knees when she heard a vehicle approaching from farther down the road. She jumped up when she saw it was a truck. Maybe the person driving it could give her—and the dead bike—a lift to the cabins.

The truck pulled over next to her. It looked nice, brand new even. *What I wouldn't give to afford a nice set of wheels.*

The driver rolled down the window and leaned out. "Need a lift?"

Their eyes connected at the same time and Lauren knew the surprise and fear on the driver's face were reflected on her own.

"Scott," she whispered. It was the only word she could get out while the pounding in her chest beat a rhythm she'd never heard.

"Lauren." Scott tipped his hat toward her and then averted his eyes. "Your parents said you were coming back."

"I just got home a couple of hours ago."

He stared straight ahead. "You gonna be around for a while?"

She shrugged. "I'm not sure how long I'll be here. I'm in the middle of a job change." Admitting to him that her Nashville dreams failed was the last thing she wanted to do.

"That's what I figured," he said. She noted the contempt in his voice. "Need a lift?"

"No. I'm fine. Just headed over to Daddy's cabins."

"That's where I'm headed. Hop in."

Lauren felt panic settling in. "That's okay. I've got my bike."

Before she could say anything else, Scott opened the door of his truck and stepped out. He'd grown since high school, adding at least three inches to his height. But that wasn't the only thing about him that changed. The skinny boy who had to cinch his pants on with a belt and a prayer while in his adolescent years had filled out. A toned, muscled version of him stood in front of her. "Whoa ..." she whispered, the word accidentally slipping from her lips.

"People change," he said with a curt nod.

She turned away from him so he wouldn't see her blush. "Really, Scott. I can get myself to the cabins, you don't need to worry about it."

"Don't be dumb. That bike isn't going anywhere and we both know it." He lifted the bike and tossed it into the back of the truck, making it look as easy as lifting a dinner plate. "Get in the truck."

Lauren shuffled her feet back and forth. Unable to think of any more excuses, she climbed into the cab. It smelled new. The ranching business must have picked up since she lived in the area.

"I can't believe you still have that bike." Scott shook his head. "I remember you pedaling all over the place on that thing."

Lauren stared out the passenger window. "I didn't know my parents kept it. You still have your blue bike?"

"The one with the lightning stripe on the side?" he asked with a laugh.

The sound of his familiar laugh tugged at her and she turned to look at him, nodding slightly.

"That got thrown out years ago—along with a lot of other crap. What happened to Betsy? I didn't think you'd ever get rid of that truck. You treated it as if it could communicate with you."

Lauren frowned. "Long story."

Silence filled the cab of the truck as they drove. Lauren knew she needed to say something, but didn't know how. She closed her eyes and cleared her throat. "I'm ... umm ... sorry about your parents. Lulu and Daddy told me what happened."

Scott didn't say anything, keeping his eyes forward and focused on the road.

"I meant to call at the time. I mean, I should have called, but ..." her words trailed off.

Three years into her stay in Nashville, Lulu called with the horrible news. Scott's dad had been diagnosed with cancer. Typical of an old rancher, he refused to go to a doctor when he started getting sick and they didn't find the tumor until it was too late to do anything. He lived for two more weeks. Devastated, Scott's mom's health deteriorated and she followed her husband to the grave only a couple short months later.

At the time, Lauren considered flying home for the second funeral, but she lacked the funds and didn't want her presence to make things worse for Scott.

Scott finally broke his silence. "I always knew I'd be the one running the ranch someday, I just didn't think it would be so soon. I only had three years of business college behind me. Had to finish the rest of the courses online while I took care of things at home, but I did it," he said with a proud lift of his chin.

"Good for you. It sounds like you're putting your degree to good use now. I mean, with the dude ranch and all."

Scott nodded, still not looking at her. "Dad used to talk about turning the place into a tourist attraction of sorts, but he never did anything about it. His dream became my dream."

Lauren didn't doubt Scott's ability to run a dude ranch. He'd always been good at organizing and entertaining. "I can't believe you convinced my parents to go in on it with you. They never change."

Scott's lips turned up slightly. "I thought they'd be a challenge, but they jumped all over it. Without them and their cabins, it would have been a pointless venture."

Scott parked his truck near the cabin rental office and climbed out. He lifted Lauren's bike from the bed of his truck and leaned it against the back of the small building.

The door opened and a petite, dark-haired woman stepped out. "Lauren Walker? Is that you?" She gasped.

Lauren grinned. "April Benson." April was the type of girl everyone knew and liked back in high school, but she never seemed to have any close friends. She'd always been a little quiet and shy.

April jumped off the porch and threw her arms around Lauren. "It's so good to see you. I don't think I've seen you since graduation."

Lauren took a moment to respond, surprised at

April's uncharacteristic reaction. "I haven't been back since graduation." She glanced at the rental office. "Are you renting a cabin?"

"Oh." April flushed. "I work for your parents. I run the front desk during the day and do the bookkeeping for them and the Double Wind. They didn't tell you?"

Lauren shook her head. *They conveniently forgot to tell me many things.*

"No problem. I'm pretty new around here. I'm sure we'll be seeing a lot of each other now that you're back."

Lauren gave her a genuine smile. "I'm glad I still know someone in this area."

Scott approached the pair from behind and April's eyes flitted to him. Lauren caught the sparkles in her eyes just before she bounced over to him. "Hey," she said, standing on tiptoes to plant a kiss on his lips.

Lauren didn't expect the reaction she felt at seeing them together. She felt herself sway and reached for something to hold onto, coming up empty.

Chapter 6

Lauren shifted from one foot to the other, trying to calm the unexpected pain building up inside her chest. *So much for having a friend in Midway. If April is connected to Scott, I can't hang out with her.*

"Are you okay?" April asked, watching Lauren's reaction.

"I'm fine. It's warm and my body's not used to this altitude anymore. Her eyes briefly fell on Scott. He seemed to be analyzing her. She averted her eyes and avoided making eye contact with either of them.

"I need to go find your dad, Lauren. I'll catch up with you two later," Scott said with another tip of his hat.

When he was out of earshot, April turned back to Lauren, concern on her face. "Are you okay with Scott and me dating? I mean, you two were together for a *really* long time. I don't want you to hate me."

"Whoa," Lauren said, putting her hands up. "Scott and I were never *together*. Yes, we were friends, but everything ended there. We never dated. Besides, I just broke up with my boyfriend of four years. I'm taking a break from guys."

April blew out her breath. "You don't know how glad I am that you're okay with this. I've been worried ever since I heard you were coming back." She tilted her head. "Now that *you're* back in town, the rest of the eligible bachelors will come out of hiding, though."

Lauren kicked at a pebble on the ground. "I won't hold my breath for that. I don't plan to be here long anyway." She stepped forward and sat down on the small porch of the rental office. "How long have you two been dating?"

"Honestly, we just started. It's only been a few weeks. We're still in that new relationship phase. At least, I am."

"Sometimes that's the only good phase of a relationship."

"True."

Lauren lifted her head. "I can't believe how much this place has changed. Nothing in my house has been moved since I left, but these cabins ... It's completely different." She tucked her knees under her chin and looked at the cabins circling the property. Two rows of twelve cabins faced each other along the long drive. Eight more cabins were scattered throughout the trees, providing more privacy to those guests who wanted it. Those cabins, including the honeymoon cabin, came at a premium.

"Your parents had each of them painted at the beginning of the summer. I think they look amazing," April said as she sat down next to Lauren.

The log cabins, once a light tan were now a deep

red with white trim around the windows and doors. "It's a nice change. They match the barn over at the Double Wind now." Lauren shielded her eyes to get a good view of the barn on the other side of the property line. "I assume that was on purpose."

"Have you been over there yet?" April asked.

Lauren shook her head.

"They cleared out the barn and built a more efficient one next to it for the horses. The old barn is where they're hosting the dinner shows each night."

"That must have taken a lot of work."

"Not as much as you'd think. They wanted to keep it authentic so they left some of the stalls and decorated them up a bit with saddles and tack and stuff. The floor is still a dirt floor, but there's now a stage built in at the opposite end." April's eyes glowed. "The place is filled with wooden picnic tables and benches that match the outside colors."

"I bet it looks great," Lauren said, trying to force emotion into her voice even though she felt numb everywhere.

April twisted a lock of hair around her finger. "I'm sorry things didn't work out for you in Nashville," she said quietly. "I know you dreamed about it for a long time."

Lauren shrugged. "That's life, I guess."

"I loved it when you performed at school activities. Do you still write your own music?"

Lauren kicked at another pebble with the toe of her shoe. "Yeah, but it still didn't get me anywhere out there."

"Is it so bad here?"

Lauren hesitated. "Only time will tell. I'll keep you

posted." She stood and brushed off the back off her jeans. "I'm going to walk around the paths through the trees a bit. I'll see ya around."

The trees behind the cabins offered shade and relief from the hot sun. Narrow trails zigged and zagged through the property until they reached the bottom of a small hill. Growing up, Lauren and her friends—usually Scott—spent a lot of time running around on the trails. In junior high, they played elaborate versions of hide and seek in the trees on weekend nights, guided only by the moonlight and the dim porch lights of the cabins.

She and Scott always won the game since they knew the trails better than anyone else. By the time they reached high school, her dad made them stop the night games. Too many guests had complained about noisy teenagers running through the woods at night.

By that time, they didn't care too much about having their games banned. They all had driver's licenses and a new world of possibilities. A short drive through the canyon and they had all of Provo and Orem to party in. Go the other direction, and they could be in Salt Lake City in less than an hour.

The snap of a twig in front of her pulled her attention back to the path she walked. A squirrel sat in the middle of the trail, staring back at her. "Hello, little fella," she said, crouching down to make herself seem less threatening.

"Hello."

She gasped and jumped up. The squirrel scampered up a nearby tree as she whirled around to meet the voice behind her.

"Sorry. I didn't mean to startle you."

Lauren stared at the unfamiliar man in front of her. "I didn't know anyone else was out here."

"I could say the same thing." He offered her a hand and she shook it hesitantly, noting his firm, confident grip. "I'm Harris. Are you a guest here, too?"

The question took her by surprise and for a moment she didn't know how to answer. "I guess in a way I am. I'm here for an extended visit."

Harris didn't stand much taller than Lauren and had close cut brown hair. His clothes looked like many of the other nature lovers that stayed at the cabins, except his appeared to be more expensive. He couldn't have been more than five years older than her.

He still held her hand in his, causing her heart to flutter. "And you are?"

"Sorry." She flushed. "My name's Lauren."

"Nice to meet you, Lauren. I have to say, this will be a hard place to leave. I only meant to stay a few days, but I ended up extending for a couple more."

"This place definitely grows on you," she said with a smile.

"Do you mind if I accompany you on your stroll through the woods or are you one who treasures solitude?"

He seems harmless and I don't want to be alone with my thoughts. "I'd love some company."

Harris fell into step next to her. "Are you staying here alone?"

Typically, meeting a stranger in the woods and having him ask her a question like that would have brought him a face full of pepper spray. But Harris didn't send off any bad vibes and asked the question like someone searching for a conversation topic.

"Actually, I'm from here in Midway. I've been living in Nashville and just got back to town." She paused. "My last name's Walker."

Harris smiled and nodded in understanding. "This is your family's place."

"Bingo."

"I've talked to your dad a couple of times since I got here. He's a great guy."

"I kind of like him."

Harris threw his head back and laughed. "Even if you didn't, I doubt you'd tell me. Did you come home to help with the opening of the Double Wind Guest Ranch?"

She shrugged. "It wasn't my intent, but the timing worked out."

Harris stared at her, nodding as if he knew exactly what she meant. "That's why I'm here. I'm a reviewer for a web-based travel company."

Lauren quickly analyzed their short conversation, wondering if she'd said anything negative that he'd use in his review. "That sounds interesting."

"I couldn't ask for a better job. I spend my time traveling the country, and sometimes the world. The places where I stay are looking for positive reviews so they up their game when I'm around. Perks galore." He winked.

"Someday I'd like to travel." She sighed.

"I've been to Nashville a couple of times. What do you do out there?"

"You can't guess?"

"Let me think." He tapped a finger on his chin and then snapped his fingers. "Artist ... wait, no ... bricklayer. Hairstylist maybe?"

Lauren tilted her head and looked at him sideways. "Try aspiring musician."

"I didn't want to go for the obvious."

"Young girl dreams of being a star, moves to Nashville for five years, only finds work as a waitress, returns home as a giant failure. My story *is* the obvious one." Lauren closed her eyes and gritted her teeth. "Sorry. I didn't mean to blurt that out. Some wounds are still raw."

"I'm sure you're an amazing musician."

"Maybe you should reserve judgment until you've heard me play or sing."

Harris stopped walking. By the time Lauren noticed, she'd already walked a few paces past him. "Are you offering?" he asked with a flirtatious smile.

She felt a blush coming on again. "Actually, it's been a while since I've performed for an audience."

"Great. I'd love to hear something."

"When do you leave town?" she asked.

"I have a plane ticket for the 3rd of July. I wanted to stick around for the grand opening and holiday dinner show the next night, but I can't swing it. I need to be in Boston before then."

"That'll give me a few days to prepare. I wouldn't want your review of the Double Wind to be a negative one because of a poorly received impromptu recital given by the owner's daughter," she said.

Harris took a step closer to her and she felt her pulse quicken. "Your performance would have to be pretty bad to sway my review. Your father and Mr. McCallister have done an excellent job with this place. If they keep it up, they're going to stay very busy … but don't tell them I said that. They'll have to wait for the review to be posted like everyone else." Harris looked down at his watch. "Speaking of work, I've got an online meeting soon. I should probably get back to my room. It was nice meeting you, Lauren. I look forward to hearing you sing."

"See ya." Lauren gave a small wave.

Harris started to walk away and then turned back. "Your dad invited me to one of their practice runs at the big barn tonight. I'm not big on dining alone in public. You wouldn't want to accompany me would you?"

Lauren lifted her eyebrows in surprise. She'd planned on attending one of the dinners at some point, but didn't think she'd be going with a date. *He seems nice enough and he'll be gone in a few days. Why not?* "Sure. I'd like that."

"Great. I'll meet you in front of the office just before seven."

She watched him walk away before resuming her walk. She followed the trails for a few more minutes before turning back and returning to the rental office. "Have you seen my dad?" she asked April.

"You just missed him. He and Scott were headed over to the big barn. Something about the entertainment. I was deep in paperwork and barely listening, though. Sorry," April answered. "You can take one of the golf carts over if you want. Like I said before, you really should see the new place. Scott's super proud of it."

"Maybe I will."

"Here ya go." April tossed her a key for the golf cart. "Don't have too much fun."

Lauren found the cart parked behind the rental

office and inserted the key. She pushed down on the pedal and the cart lurched forward. She missed the four-wheelers they used to have.

She and Scott once got his dad's four wheeler stuck in the mud after a spring rainstorm. By the time they dug it out, there wasn't a spot on either of them not covered in goop. Rather than dwell on the negative, they jumped back into the mud, knowing it might be their only chance to literally roll around in the mud. When they got back to the ranch, Scott's mom made them hose off before they were allowed in the barn, let alone the house. Lauren shivered at the thought of the cold hose water. Despite the frigid shower, it had been one of her most memorable afternoons.

The path from the cabin rentals to the Double Wind buildings used to be nothing more than a horse trail, but it had been improved to a narrow gravel road. The wheels of the cart crunched over the rocks as she approached the barn. Just like the cabins, it had a new coat of dark red paint and white trim.

"Hello?" Lauren called, knocking on the side of the open barn doors. It took her eyes a second to adjust to the light as she entered the large room.

"Over here!" She recognized her dad's voice.

"Wow," she breathed as she wove through the picnic tables to the back of the building where a large stage had been built. "April wasn't kidding. This place is amazing."

Scott stood on the edge of the stage, but still avoided looking at her straight on when answering. "It's come a long way from the days when you were here."

"That's an understatement." She looked up at the ceiling, stretching her neck. Rope lights wrapped around the long beams of the roof, providing a glow that filled the room. "Did you raise the roof?"

"Nope. We just took down the loft since no one used it anyway."

"Right. I forgot about it."

"What do you think of our stage?" her dad asked. "Does it rival those fancy ones you're used to?"

"It's close."

"Built it ourselves."

Lauren raised her eyebrows. "Really? I didn't know either of you had carpentry skills."

"A little bit of blood, sweat, and tears and this is what we got," Scott said with a wave of his hand. He finally looked at her head on and she felt her heart flutter as it filled with emotion.

"So what kind of entertainment will you have?" she said, stepping closer to her dad.

"We're opening with a cowboy poet," her dad answered. "He sings and plays the guitar, too. He'll be here at least through this first summer season."

Lauren nodded. "Sounds ... entertaining."

"You're welcome to come to tonight's dinner. There's no entertainment yet, but you can try out our food."

Lauren hesitated. "Actually, someone already invited me."

"Someone?" her dad asked with a raise of his brows.

Lauren glanced at Scott. He'd knelt down and was messing with a cluster of wires. She didn't know if he was even listening, but his jaw clenched and unclenched multiple times.

"I was talking to one of the cabin guests, Harris, and he asked me to join him tonight. He didn't want to come alone."

"Harris? The guy who's here to *review* this place?" Scott gave her a look filled with surprise and a hint of anger.

"He mentioned that was his reason for the visit."

"Maybe you could talk the place up while you're eating," her dad said with a smile. Nothing ever got to him.

"Hmm... What would *I* get out of that deal?" she joked, fully knowing that Harris had already decided to give the ranch a favorable review.

"How about a free meal tonight and room and board until you can afford your own place?"

"Ouch."

Her dad put his arm around her and squeezed. "You know we love having you back."

"Uh huh. I should probably get back to the house. I'm sure Lulu could use some help with ... something."

She started to walk away, but her dad stopped her. "Hold on a sec." He turned and whispered something to Scott. In turn, Scott shrugged and returned to the wires he'd been messing with. "How would you feel about being our guinea pig tonight?"

"Guinea pig?"

"Hal, our cowboy poet, won't get into town for another day or two. We want to make sure we have this sound system set up correctly before he gets here. Maybe you could play and sing a song or two tonight. You know, to test our wiring skills."

Lauren glanced at Scott. His mouth was drawn in a

straight line, not giving away his true feelings. "I guess I could do that." She chewed on her lip.

"Really? We'd appreciate it. You're no stranger to the stage. I didn't think you'd mind."

I don't mind, except that it will remind me exactly how far I've fallen from where I thought I'd be. And I'm pretty sure Scott doesn't want me on his stage. "Do you mind if I take the golf cart home, Daddy? I'm kind of stranded here."

"That's fine. They get moved from place to place anyway."

"Thanks. I'll see you tonight then. See ya, Scott."

Scott waved, but kept his head down.

Times have definitely changed. It's as if we barely know each other. I'm not sure which of us is to blame. Maybe a little of both. It doesn't matter, though. After what happened, we can't go back to the way things were before.

Chapter 7

Lauren flopped onto the pink bedspread in her room and stared at the ceiling. She knew she should practice something for the dinner show that night, but she couldn't bring herself to do it. Her biggest performance in five years and it would be for twenty people in her ex-friend's barn. *Yay. I've finally arrived in the big time.*

The smell of baking bread wafted up the stairs and under her bedroom door. Her stomach growled. "At least I'll get a good meal out of it," she mumbled as she climbed off the bed and knelt on the floor in front of her suitcases.

She spent the rest of the afternoon packing up old mementos and unpacking her current things. Finally, at six o'clock, she pulled on a clean pair of jeans and tied her hair up with a pink bow to match her pink boots. She'd skip the cowboy hat that night. After all, she wouldn't want to overdo it with Harris watching.

Her parents had already left by the time she

wandered downstairs. She opened her violin case and carefully turned the pegs of the instrument. Hundreds of miles bouncing around in the cab of her truck had left it horribly out of tune. She fingered the strings, but didn't play anything.

Outside, she carefully tucked the violin case into the back of the golf cart and strapped it in as if it were a set of clubs. "Not sure why I bothered tuning it before I left the house," she mumbled out loud as she bounced down the long driveway.

The heat of the day had lessened by that time of night, but the sun still shone bright in the sky as she drove past the rental cabins. A night attendant, someone she'd never met, had replaced April in the office. Instead of introducing herself and making small talk, she sat outside on one of the wicker rocking chairs and waited for Harris. He showed up a few minutes later dressed in a button-up shirt with a sport coat.

She looked down at her jeans and cringed. "I think I'm underdressed."

He sat in the rocking chair next to hers. "On the contrary, I think I'm the one who's overdressed. This *is* a dude ranch after all."

Lauren pointed toward the golf cart. "Are you ready to go? I called a limo in for the night."

Harris grinned. "A girl who likes nice things. You're my kind of woman."

Lauren blushed as she climbed into the driver's seat of the cart. "Hold on tight, I'm just learning to drive this thing. And it goes soooo," she drew out the word, "fast."

"What's with the case?" Harris asked as he leaned

over the back of the seat.

"It's my violin. I've been recruited to test the sound system tonight."

Harris raised his eyebrows. "I get a show after all?"

"If you could call it that. I'll just play or sing a couple songs. No big deal."

"I look forward to it," he said as they arrived at the barn. He put a hand on her waist and steered her toward the entrance.

The feel of his hand made her nervous and she shied away, pretending to readjust the instrument case in her hand.

Inside the barn, the smell of barbecue chicken and baked beans mingled with that of the fresh bread. If it tasted anything like it smelled, the Double Wind would have a hit on their hands even if the entertainment lacked pizzazz.

Lulu waved them over to the serving tables as soon as they entered the building. "Welcome to the Double Wind. Dinner is served in a chow line and seating is first come, first served." She leaned in to Harris and cupped her hand over her mouth. "I'd suggest sitting near the front for the best view of tonight's show."

Lauren rolled her eyes, but after their plates were filled to the brim with hot food, Harris led her to a table in the front row—right in the center of the stage. Scott stood on the stage in front of the table, adjusting the microphone.

"I hope you're not disappointed," she remarked to Harris.

He leaned closer to her. "I doubt you ever

disappoint."

She blushed and turned away, catching a glimpse of Scott as she did so. He gritted his teeth and stalked off the stage. *What's his problem?*

Harris shoveled a forkful of food into his mouth before closing his eyes and sighing. "I think I've died and gone to heaven. Got any connections so I can snag an invitation to all the practice dinners before I leave?"

"I might know a person or two who can help with that," Lauren answered with a smile.

Harris was right. Scott's ranch hand had outdone himself with the cooking, and Lulu's bread tasted as good as it always did. The other guests, none of which she recognized, chatted easily at their individual tables. Conversation with Harris came easily. He liked to flirt, but she knew he didn't mean anything by it—a fact that gave her some relief.

Too soon, her dad caught her eye from across the room. *"You're on!"* he mouthed.

She excused herself from the table and headed to the side of the stage where she'd stowed her violin. She tuned it again and gave a nod to Scott standing at the microphone.

"Welcome to the Double Wind Guest Ranch," Scott said. "Tonight we have a surprise treat for everyone in attendance. Our regular dinner shows will begin on the 4th of July, so make sure you come back for that, but in the meantime, we have a special guest tonight. All the way from Nashville, Tennessee, give a warm welcome to Lauren Walker!"

Applause filled the barn, echoing off the high ceiling. Hearing the sound reminded her how much she'd missed performing for groups and she smiled as her body and mind came to life again. She walked across the stage with confidence and gripped the microphone. "Thank you Mr. McCallister and thank *you*," she motioned to the audience, "for that welcome. It's been a long time since I've performed around here and I'm happy to be here tonight." She let go of the microphone and lifted her violin into the air. "I'm going to open with a fiddling piece I think you might like."

She took a step back and lifted the instrument to her neck. Closing her eyes, she took a deep breath and then opened her eyes again as she launched into the song. She danced and tapped her feet while she played, getting more into the music as the audience began to stomp their feet and clap in rhythm with the music. Finally, she ended the tune with a long drawn out note and a dramatic lift of her bow.

The applause, much louder than in the beginning, boosted her spirits and she grinned as she approached the microphone again. "Thank you so much. I'm glad you liked that. Would you like to hear me sing?"

The audience cheered and she nodded to Scott who started a soundtrack offstage. She sang two lively songs before picking up her violin again and playing a final fiddling tune. "Thanks for your support tonight. And don't forget to come back to the Double Wind later this summer to experience the fun of Hal the cowboy poet."

Lauren started to walk away, but Harris jumped up from the table in front of the stage and yelled "Encore! Encore!" before she made it halfway to the steps. Embarrassed, she turned and bowed to the crowd before continuing her walk across the stage.

Harris continued to yell.

Not sure what to do, she glanced at Scott for help. He shrugged and put his hands up as if to say he didn't want anything to do with it. She turned around and returned to the microphone. "I guess I can sing one more song if you'd like."

Harris whistled.

"This song is one I wrote myself. There's no accompaniment with it yet, so bear with me."

She gripped the microphone with both hands and began to sing. It was the same song she sang when she auditioned to be a backup singer for the Tennessee Boots band. The song told the story of a girl—her—chasing her dreams and fighting to fulfill them. The crowd listened in silence as the evocative melody and her soothing voice filled the barn.

Halfway through the song, Scott got up and stalked out of the building. It surprised her and she faltered, but quickly regained her composure and finished it perfectly. Back at the table, Harris gushed over her performance.

"That was amazing," he said. "You act modest, but you've got talent. Real talent. Remind me why you left Nashville?"

"Apparently no one out there saw in me what you see," she said wryly.

"The Double Wind should just hire you as their permanent entertainment."

To be honest, that same thought had crossed her mind while she stood on the stage. She looked toward the doors where Scott had disappeared during her final song. "It would never work."

"Too bad. People will miss out."

She gave him a gracious smile. "Thanks. It's nice to know I haven't completely lost my touch."

They finished their dinner, scooping every last drop of vanilla ice cream with raspberry sauce out of their bowls before sitting back in their chairs and sighing.

"I have an early conference call," Harris said. "I should get back to my cabin."

"I'll drive you," Lauren said. "The golf cart doesn't turn back into a pumpkin for another hour."

Harris chuckled. "Thanks for the offer, but I think I'll just walk. I need the exercise and I love the evening air here in the mountains." He took her hand and kissed it softly before standing and walking out the door.

As soon as Harris disappeared out the doors, Lulu hurried over to Lauren's table. "Well?"

"Well, what?" Lauren feigned ignorance.

"How'd we do?"

"I think he liked it."

"You *think*? Did he give any indication on what he might say in the review?"

Lauren squinted her eyes and pretended to be deep in thought. "Nope. Not that I can think of. He's a real mystery, that one."

Lulu's worry lines creased. "Did you at least talk us up?"

"I did nothing but talk about the ranch while we ate."

Lulu didn't catch her joking tone and kept talking. "I think it was smart of Dad and Scott to have you play tonight. Harris seemed to like it. It had to have helped our rating."

"I don't know about that, he commented about a couple out-of-tune notes I hit."

Lulu's eyes widened. "Really?"

"No, Lulu. I'm sure he'll give you a fine review. Do you need any extra help cleaning up?"

Lulu shook her head. "No need. We've got staff to do it."

"I guess I should be getting home then. It's a long drive in a golf cart and I'll be getting up early to clean cabins since I'm once again a maid."

Lulu cringed. "I wish you wouldn't say it like that. You used to like working in the cabins."

Lauren shrugged. "That was before I had a taste of independence."

Chapter 8

W ake up, sleepyhead," a soft voice whispered. Lauren opened her eyes and then quickly shut them again as the bright light from her overhead fixture shone down. She felt the pink and white bedspread being pulled from her body and opened her eyes again, squinting that time.

Lulu's face appeared over her, just inches away. "Time to get up. Wouldn't want you to be late to work this morning."

Lauren rolled over and looked at her alarm clock. "I have plenty of time."

"I know it's hard for you to get up in the mornings."

"Maybe when I was a teenager. I'm perfectly capable of getting myself up now. I set my alarm." As if on cue, the alarm next to her head began to beep and she reached over and smacked it to turn it off. "See?"

"Good for you." Lulu patted her arm. "I'll be downstairs making breakfast. Any requests?"

"I'm not really hungry. I'll just grab a granola bar on the way out."

"That's no way to start a morning," Lulu said. "I'll make pancakes and bacon."

Lauren crawled out of bed and tugged her t-shirt down. "Mom, I'm fine. I can take care of myself," she snapped.

Lulu put up her hands. "I'm just trying to help."

Lauren closed her eyes and took a deep breath. "I know, but I'm not in high school anymore. I'm an adult. I should be taking care of you now."

"What are you saying? I'm not that old and decrepit yet." lulu smiled. "Fine. I won't make you breakfast, but I did start a load of laundry for you." She hurried out of the bedroom before Lauren had a chance to say anything else.

At the cabins, Lauren once again parked the golf cart behind the rental office. Having worked as a housekeeper for her parents in the past, she knew to wear comfortable shoes and old clothes. She pulled a hair tie off her wrist and twisted her hair on top of her head, securing it with the tie. Not the most flattering look, but it didn't matter for the job she'd be doing.

"Morning, Lauren," April greeted her when she walked through the front door.

"Good morning. Do you have a list of which cabins need prepped?"

April patted a piece of paper on the desk in front of her. "Right here. First, I need you to fill out the new employee forms, though."

Lauren raised her eyebrows. "New employee

forms?"

"Yeah, so we can get everything right on your paychecks, you know, taxes and deductions and all that."

"Oh." Lauren tried to swallow her pride.

"When you're done, you can just hand them to me and I'll take care of the rest. The new time clock is hanging by the back door. There's a card with your name on it to punch."

"Thanks." Lauren took the stack of papers April offered and sat down in a chair to fill them out. She'd assumed her parents would pay her in cash like they did when she was growing up. They were taking the guest ranch thing seriously. She wondered how much was them and how much was Scott's influence. Either way, she was sufficiently humiliated.

The only sound that could be heard in the office was the scratching of Lauren's pencil across the paper. After a few moments, April cleared her throat. "I feel bad that I'm over you now. I mean, this is *your* parents' place. You should be the one sitting behind the desk and I should be the one cleaning up other people's messes."

Lauren looked up. Genuine concern filled April's eyes. "Trust me, you're much better suited to that job than me. I know nothing about bookkeeping and all that paperwork stuff."

April nodded slightly. "I did get an accounting degree. I didn't think I'd use it much, though. I planned to get married and stay home with my babies. Someday, maybe."

Lauren stood and returned the papers to April. "I'm sure it won't be long." *I just hope I'm not around to witness it if Scott's the father.*

She took the list of cabins needing housekeeping and left the building. A small room with a rolling housekeeping cart and two jumbo washers and dryers was attached to the back of the building. She turned the key in the lock and stepped back as she opened it. The smell of cleaning supplies assailed her senses, bringing back a barrage of memories—some good, some bad.

Unlike a traditional hotel, they only offered housekeeping service at the beginning and end of a stay. The guests maintained their own cabins while there. If they needed extra supplies, they left word at the rental office. That morning eight of the thirty cabins needed prepped for new guests checking in by the end of the day.

Lauren set to work, stripping beds and putting on clean sheets, scrubbing bathrooms, and sweeping the wood floors. It had been years since she did work like that. She could only imagine how sore she'd be if her feet and muscles weren't already used to a lot of movement from being a waitress for five years.

Just as she finished the last room, Harris stepped out of his cabin. He stood on his front porch in bare feet and watched her while he sipped from the mug in his hands. She smiled and waved.

"Beautiful day," he called.

She wheeled her cart over to his porch. "Definitely can't complain."

He reached out and touched her hair tied up on the top of her head, twisting a lock between his fingers. His flirting seemed to be escalating.

"After seeing you perform last night, I can't believe

this is what you do for a living," he said.

"It's only temporary. Besides, what's wrong with being a housekeeper?"

"I only meant that your talents are being wasted," he said defensively.

"Not all of us can travel the country being pampered."

He threw his head back and laughed. "True, true. I'm definitely spoiled. You can always come with me, be my assistant or something."

Lauren leaned closer to him. "Don't tempt me." She looked down at her cart. "Until I'm whisked away, I've got laundry to do. I'll see ya around."

Harris nodded to her and stepped back inside his cabin. She returned to the housekeeping room and stuffed the dirty linens into the machines. Until they were done washing, she had a little free time on her hands. She thought about walking the trails behind the cabins again, but decided to head back to the office. She'd been away from the Midway rumor mill for five years. Maybe April could catch her up on people and places.

She pushed the door of the office open but stopped halfway over the threshold. Scott leaned against the desk behind the counter, one hand on April's shoulder. They seemed to be having a private conversation.

"Sorry," Lauren mumbled as she backed out the screen door, tripping over her feet in the process.

"Wait!" April called. "Come back."

Embarrassed, Lauren entered again but kept her eyes on the desk.

"We were just chatting. Did you finish the cabins?"

April said.

"Yeah, just waiting for the wash to finish."

April turned to Scott. "You should take Lauren with you."

"I don't think she—" Scott started to say something but April cut him off.

"Scott found a section of fence that needed mending while taking one of the guests on a ride this morning. He's headed out to repair it. You should go with him."

Lauren eyed April suspiciously. No sane person would send another woman to hang out with her boyfriend. "I don't have a horse."

"Have you seen how many they have over at the Double Wind now? There're plenty. Seriously, go with him."

It had been five years since she'd been on a horse and the idea sounded enticing, but the frown on Scott's face and the tenseness in his shoulders worried her.

"Want to?" was all he said.

"Uhh ... sure. I guess. I can finish washing the bedding later. We won't need it tonight anyway."

"Let's go." He lightly kissed April—Lauren looked away—and then stepped out the office door without saying anything else.

Lauren held back. "Are you sure about this?"

"All I know is that the two of you used to be friends. Now, it's as if you are complete strangers. I have no idea what happened between you and I don't need to know, but I don't like seeing two of my friends hurt. Maybe if you spend some time together, you can work out whatever's wrong."

"I'm willing to forgive and forget, but I don't know if he is," Lauren confided.

"It's worth a shot."

When Lauren walked out of the office, Scott was already halfway up the road to the barns and she had to hurry to catch up. "I don't have to come with you, you know," she said as she trotted beside him.

He shrugged. "Doesn't matter much."

"You *used* to care if I was around or not."

Scott stopped in his tracks. "We were young. Kids even. A lot has changed."

"So you're saying you don't want me to come." Lauren tried not to let the hurt she felt inside come out in her voice.

He kicked at the dirt with his boots. "I'm saying it doesn't make a difference to me."

Lauren gritted her teeth. "I'm coming, but not for you. I haven't ridden a horse in a long time and I miss it. That's all."

"Good."

"Good," she snapped.

Scott turned back to the road and continued his fast pace to the new barn. Lauren kept pace a few steps behind, trying to keep her seething to a minimum.

The new barn consisted of twelve stalls with a large tack room in the front. The back doors opened into a large corral and exercise arena. "Whoa," Lauren breathed when she saw it. "This is nice."

"Dad started this part before he died," Scott said quietly. "Too bad he never got to see it finished."

Lauren ran her hands along the wood rails as she walked from stall to stall. Each had a silver plaque with a horse's name engraved on the front. "Do you have to take care of all this alone?"

"I have two other full-time ranch hands here at the property, two who keep track of the cattle, and a few part timers who come teach classes periodically."

"I'm impressed."

"Thanks." For the first time that day, she got a smile out of him. Her heart fluttered ... just a bit.

Lauren stopped at one of the stalls and read the plaque. "Minnow," she whispered. "Is this the same Minnow that was just a colt when we graduated?"

Scott walked over to her. "She's one and the same."

"I remember sitting on the fence and watching your dad try to break her to the saddle."

Scott laughed. "She was pretty spirited back then. She's changed. Probably our gentlest horse. Want to ride her?"

Lauren reached her hand out to the brown and white horse who happily let her rub her hand along her soft back. "I'd love to."

After saddling their horses and leading them from the barn, Lauren waited while Scott gathered and tied fencing equipment to his horse's saddlebags. "You still remember how to get on one of these, right?" he teased.

She glared at him and easily swung herself onto the horse. "Just like riding a bike," she said. *Of course, he's already rescued me and my bike since I've been back.*

Scott shook his head. "You've already forgotten at least one important thing."

She looked down at the reins in her hands and her

feet in the stirrups. "What? What am I missing?"

He dismounted and tied his horse to the fence. "Hold on a sec," he said before disappearing into the tack room again.

He returned with a cowboy hat in his hands. Reaching up, he helped her down from Minnow's back. "Good thing I have a supply of these for the city girls who want to look like they're authentic cowgirls."

Lauren put her hands on her hips. "I've got plenty of hats, thank you very much. I just don't find it easy to clean cabins while wearing one. When I left the house, I had no idea I'd be going riding today."

Scott looked at her feet. "That explains your choice in footwear, too, I guess."

She stared at her old tennis shoes. "Can't clean bathrooms in boots."

He reached up and pulled the hair tie from her hair. Her brown hair cascaded down her back. For a brief moment, her breath caught in her throat as he stuck the hat on her head and adjusted it. She hadn't been that close to him in a long time and the smell of him brought memories crashing back. She closed her eyes and leaned into his hand, inhaling his scent. His fingers twitched ever so slightly and she opened her eyes.

He dropped his hand. "Sorry." He untied his horse and swung himself up with one hand. "Let's go."

Chapter 9

Although her parents never owned horses, Lauren had spent enough time on the McCallisters' horses growing up to be considered a good rider. It only took a few minutes atop Minnow to feel comfortable in the saddle again. She relaxed and enjoyed the breeze on her face as Minnow trotted alongside Scott and his horse.

"Besides Minnow, what other horses do you still have that I'd remember?" Lauren asked.

Scott creased his eyebrows. "All of them, I think. Except Sunshine. She died a couple of years ago."

"She was ancient."

"You could say that. The new horses are all chosen by temperament rather than speed or looks. Don't want any guests complaining about bucking, runaway horses."

Lauren turned in the saddle to look at him. "I imagine some of the guests have never ridden a horse before."

"Oh, the stories I could tell after only a few months of business." He smiled halfway and shook his head. "One woman who was," he cleared his throat, "particularly large in stature, insisted on putting the opposite foot in the stirrup every time she tried to mount. Three times in a row she swung herself onto the saddle only to find herself facing her horse's rump."

Lauren giggled. "How did you keep your composure?"

Scott grinned—the impish grin she hadn't seen for five years."It was a struggle, that's for sure. The worst part was trying to get her back down every time she did that."

Lauren closed her eyes and took a deep breath, inhaling the clean mountain air as far into her lungs as she could. "I missed the outdoors."

"Really? Miss I'm-Too-Good-For-Small-Town-Living got homesick?" Scott teased.

She opened her eyes again. "I didn't say that. But, there's something about this place that gets under your skin."

Scott turned from side to side, taking in as much of the view as he could from atop his horse. "I could never leave. Being away for college was torture. I came home for every break."

She tilted her head at him. "Don't you have any desire to see the world? Learn new things? Explore?"

"Of course. I'd love that ... as long as I could always come back here."

They arrived at the section of damaged fence and dismounted. Lauren sat in the grass and leaned against a fencepost while Scott worked. Neither said much, content to enjoy the peacefulness in silence.

When Scott finished, he sat down next to her and took off his hat, wiping the sweat from his brow. "Record breaking heat this summer, they say."

"Feels like it," Lauren said without looking up. She had picked a pile of tiny purple wildflowers and sat twisting their stems together, forming a wreath. "I can only imagine how warm it is down in the valleys."

Scott watched her work in silence. His presence made her nervous. In the five years she'd spent away, she thought she'd gotten over losing his friendship, yet his proximity to her that day unnerved her. When he reached over and took the wreath from her, their hands brushed against each other. Her heart fluttered.

"I remember you making these all the time when we were kids," he said. "You'd twist them together and I'd give them to Lulu."

Lauren smiled at the memory. "There was a reason for that. Every time we gave her flowers she fed us pie or cookies or bread."

"Mmm ... delicious." He rubbed his stomach and then stood. "We should probably get back. We have another dinner planned for tonight." He grabbed two water bottles from his horse's saddlebags and tossed one to her.

She took one last look around their place of solitude and blew out her breath. She'd been trying to gather the courage to speak to him and didn't know when she'd get another perfect chance. "Scott," she began. "I'm sorry for the way things went down when I left. I never thought this ... this feud, for lack of a better word ... would continue for as long as it did. Maybe we can start over. If we're going to be seeing a lot of each other, I'd rather it not be awkward. I miss *us.*"

Scott gave one nod of his head. "Agreed. We're both different people. We can be mature about this."

"Right."

"Right."

They both smiled at each other and then laughed. For the first time in weeks Lauren felt like something in her life wasn't crashing down.

"How was your first day back on the job?" Lulu asked when Lauren walked through the front door late that afternoon.

"I'd forgotten how tiring the job can be. And after working as a full-time waitress, that's saying something." Lauren flopped onto one of the barstools and rested her head on her arms.

"Try kneading bread dough every day. My arms have gotten stronger just since we started doing the dinners last week." She flexed her biceps and pursed her lips together as if straining to make them bigger.

"Not bad for a woman your age," Lauren said and then ducked to avoid the wet rag thrown at her.

Lulu picked up the rag and turned her attention to the sink. "Dad said you and Scott went riding today."

"He was mending fence. I went with him." She drummed her fingers on the counter.

"It's good to see you two talking. I'm tired of walking on eggshells when it comes to both of you."

Lauren raised her eyebrows. "I haven't even been around."

"I know, but the last time I mentioned him while

you were in Nashville, you asked me not to talk about him anymore," Lulu whispered as if sharing a guarded secret.

"I forgot about that. Sorry."

"No harm now."

Lauren chewed on her lip. "He and April make a cute couple."

Lulu shrugged. "They're alright."

"You don't think so?" she asked in surprise.

"They're cute, I just don't know if they're right for each other."

"Oh." *Not sure what she means.*

"Anyway, I need to get the bread over to the ranch for the dinner. Are you coming tonight?"

"I didn't plan to. I need to catch up on sleep."

"Good. Then you won't mind if I take the golf cart you drove."

"Not at all. The key's still in it."

Lauren made herself a small dinner and took it to the back porch to eat. From there, she could see Scott's home across her yard and their back fences. She found herself thinking about him more than she wanted to. The way he smelled, the way he touched her hair, the way he smiled at her. It took years of living in Nashville before she stopped trying to call him or text him every time something funny or exciting happened. Even with Brendan in her life for four of those years, she couldn't put Scott from her mind.

"He has April now. Even if you wanted something more, it couldn't happen," she said aloud. "Don't butt into their lives."

Lauren's cell phone vibrated in her pocket and she

pulled it out. The number on the screen didn't look familiar and she didn't recognize the area code. Usually she let that type of call go to voicemail, but that night she felt adventurous.

"Hello?" she answered.

"Lauren?"

"This is she."

"Hi. This is Harris. I hope you don't mind me calling. Your mom gave me your number earlier today."

"I don't mind."

"When I go to new towns, I sample local cuisine and attend local events so I can add those to my reviews of hotels and resorts. Tonight I'm riding the Heber Creeper and I noticed there's a couple's package. Would you be interested in coming with me?"

She stared at her half-eaten dinner. "That sounds fun. I haven't ridden the train in years."

"Great. They're doing a chocolate tasting on board tonight."

"Who doesn't love chocolate?"

"Exactly." Harris laughed. *"Did you want to meet me at my cabin?"*

"Umm ... I don't actually have a vehicle right now." She closed her eyes in embarrassment even though he couldn't see her.

"No problem. Give me your address and I'll come pick you up. I've got a rental car. Will fifteen minutes be okay?"

Lauren looked down at her clothes. She still wore the same dirty jeans and t-shirt she wore at work and to go riding with Scott. "Fifteen minutes is fine."

As soon as she hung up, she ran into the house and up the stairs, two at a time. No time for a shower, so extra deodorant and perfume would have to suffice. She threw on a clean sundress and scrubbed her face, reapplying her makeup in record time. There wasn't much she could do with her long hair except brush through it. Harris rang the doorbell just as she finished buckling a pair of blue sandals.

"What? No boots tonight?" Harris said, pretending to be shocked.

"Sometimes my feet need a break."

He led her to his car and opened the door for her. They didn't lack for conversation. As soon as he buckled next to her she pumped him for information about his job. She wanted to know all about the places he'd been, the things he'd seen, and the people he'd met. She continued her string of questions even after they arrived in Heber City, a few miles from Midway, and boarded the train.

"You weren't joking when you said you wanted to travel," Harris finally said with a wink.

"Not at all. Of course, the fear of never getting to see all these places is what makes it so urgent now."

Harris stared out the window as the train rounded the curves around Deer Creek Reservoir. The setting sun sent a rainbow of color across the water. "Lauren, I have a proposition for you, but I don't want you to take it the wrong way."

She raised her eyebrows. "Okay ..."

"I'm doing this as a friend, and I don't expect anything for it."

"My curiosity is thoroughly piqued." *Should I be worried about what's about to happen?*

"I fly out to Boston the day after tomorrow."

"You mentioned that the other day."

"I'll be there for a two-night stay, reviewing a new hotel. After that, I have back-to-back resorts booked. They're supposed to be fabulous and have full-service spas on site. Anyway, I thought it might be fun to have a female view added to mine. After all, I can't judge a manicure as well as someone like say … you."

Lauren's jaw dropped. "Are you asking me to come with you?"

Harris nodded once. "The first resort is in North Carolina near the Outer Banks. The second one is really fancy. They'll pull out all the stops. Ever been to Myrtle Beach?"

Lauren shook her head back and forth. "You're joking with me, right?"

"Not at all. I even ran it by my boss. He thought it was a great idea. If the resorts agree to comp a room for you, too—which I have no doubt they will—you're more than welcome to join me. Who knows, you might like it so much that you find yourself a new career."

"Would I get paid?"

"Not for the first two. If you joined the company you would, of course."

"I don't know what to say." Lauren's mind raced.

"It will be fun. Pampering and entertainment all paid for by the resorts. It will be a week and a half of fun with no strings attached."

"It's sounds amazing. I just … I've only been back home for a couple days."

Harris leaned closer to her. "I'll tell you what, think about it tonight and you can give me your answer tomorrow."

"Thanks, I will."

Harris's offer to travel the country sounded

enticing, but Lauren couldn't help but feel like she'd be running away from her problems if she agreed to the plan. As hard as she'd tried, she'd failed so far in adult life. *Leaving just when I'm attempting to get back on my feet would be like throwing in the towel. Wouldn't it?*

But he did say it might lead to a permanent job ...

After the train ride and a stop for ice cream at a local favorite in Heber City, Lauren climbed out of Harris's car and waved goodbye to him from her driveway. She glanced down at her cell. Just past one o'clock. She jumped when she opened her front door and saw her dad sitting on the couch in the living room.

"Daddy? Why are you still up?" She looked at the clock on the wall, wondering if she'd misread the time on her phone.

"Do you have any idea what time it is?" he said quietly.

"Yeah. It's a quarter after one."

Lulu came down the stairs in her bathrobe and sat on a middle stair. "Do you know how worried we've been?"

Lauren looked at them with confusion. "I left a note on the kitchen counter. Didn't you see it?"

"Yes, we saw it," Lulu snapped. She'd never been able to stay as calm as her husband.

"I don't understand what the problem is," Lauren said with narrowed eyes.

"The problem is that you left with an almost stranger and stayed out half the night. Curfew is midnight."

"*Excuse me?*" Lauren squeaked. "I'm an adult. I

haven't had a curfew since high school."

"Maybe you've been doing crazy things in Nashville, but now that you're back here, under our roof, there's no reason to stay out that late," her father said, still in his calm, quiet voice.

Lauren shook her head in disbelief. "I'm at a complete loss for words. I can't stay here if I'm going to be treated like a child." She moved toward the staircase. "Harris wanted me to travel with him, visit a couple resorts. I figured I'd turn him down, but I think you've just changed my mind."

She stepped over Lulu and ran up the stairs, slamming the door to her room.

Chapter 10

The next morning, Lauren got up early and left the house before her parents came down. She wasn't ready to deal with them yet. She took the golf cart parked next to her dad's truck by the garage, hoping he wouldn't need it. Since she arrived at the rental cabins earlier than anyone would be leaving, she parked the cart behind the office and went for a walk along the trails behind the cabins.

Thoughts of her current situation filled her mind. Choices and decisions flashed through her brain as she walked, trying to come up with a solution to her problems. *My parents are so frustrating. I'm an adult and have been for a long time. Why can't they see it? Is it because I had a run of bad luck? Even people their age have bad years. And should I go with Harris? I'll see places I've never seen before and it won't cost me a cent. Of course, if I leave, my parents will hire someone to replace me and then I'll be in the same boat I was in when I got to Midway. Unless I enjoy writing reviews and Harris follows through with getting me a job with his company… That would be nice, but I'd never have a place to call home. Do I even want a place to call home?*

After an hour of walking, she returned to the office.

"Morning, April," Lauren said as she entered through the back door.

"Good morning." April tilted her head and looked at Lauren. "You okay?"

"I'm fine."

"You seem … tired. Or maybe stressed."

"I've got a lot to think about."

"I'm here if you want to talk. I'm serious."

Lauren smiled at her. "Thanks. I appreciate that."

She cleaned the cabins with vigor that morning. Only four of the tenants were checking out that day so it didn't take long to clean the rooms and replace the linens. The next day would be much busier with half the guests leaving and their places being filled with new people.

Every time she stepped outside to get something off her housekeeping cart, she glanced at Harris's cabin. The curtains were drawn and the lights off. She knew she wouldn't be able to avoid him all day. He'd need an answer soon, especially if the answer was yes.

"That was quick," April said when she returned to the office.

"I clean fast when I'm preoccupied with other things," Lauren said with a half smile.

April leaned on the counter. "Scott just radioed over. He wants me to prepare new employee papers for the cowboy poet. Hal just got to the ranch and

Scott's pretty busy. Any chance you'd be willing to take the forms up to the Double Wind and save him a trip over here?"

Lauren glanced out the window. Still no sign of life from Harris's cabin. "Sure. I can do that. I've got nothing else to do today."

She sat in a chair while April prepared the documents and stuffed them in a manila envelope. "Tell Scott that Hal can return these anytime before the first performance on the 4th of July."

"Will do. Anything else?"

April grinned. "Try to smile."

Lauren fought it back but she laughed and a smile crossed her face. "Thanks. Sometimes I need a little reminding."

She stepped out the back door and into the golf cart. The little vehicle was starting to feel more like home than her own bedroom back at the farmhouse. She missed Betsy. The two hundred dollars she got for parts after Betsy's engine blew in Colorado didn't make up for the loss of her independence.

At the Double Wind she stopped at the horse barn first, but no one was inside. Six of the stalls were empty and she wondered if Scott had taken a group out on a ride. She set the envelope down and stuck her hand through the slats in Minnow's stall. "Hey, girl. It's good to see you again," she whispered as she petted the horse's nose. "Do you think Scott will let me ride you again sometime? I didn't realize how much I missed it. And you were a perfect lady yesterday."

"Can I help you?" a voice spoke behind her.

She turned her head to see a teenage boy with a

tuft of dark hair standing up in back. He struggled to carry one of the large saddles. A nametag was pinned to his shirt, but she wasn't close enough to read what it said. *Must be one of the new hires.* "I'm looking for Scott. Have you seen him?"

"Scott? Is he another guest here?" He shifted his feet to readjust the weight of the saddle he carried. "I haven't met all the guests yet."

Lauren smiled. "Scott's the owner."

"Oh! Sorry. I only know him as Mr. McCallister. I think he's in the show barn." He let the saddle fall to the ground and pointed through the barn doors at the building that held the nightly dinner shows.

"Thanks," she took a step closer to read his nametag, "Jesse."

"No problem, Ma'am. I'm here to help."

She chuckled to herself as she picked up the envelope and left the horse barn. At the show barn, she pushed the heavy doors aside. Inside, it was dark and quiet. "Scott! Hello?" she called. No answer. "Scott!" Still nothing.

She whirled around at the sound of footsteps behind her.

"Looking for someone?" a man asked.

"I'm looking for Scott McCallister."

"You just missed him."

"Thanks, Mr. ...?"

"Boomer. Hal Boomer."

Lauren lifted her eyebrows. "You're the cowboy poet."

The man, who looked to be in his late fifties, took off his hat and bowed dramatically. "At your service. Apparently, my reputation precedes me. Should I be flattered that you've heard of me or concerned?"

"Flattered," Lauren said as she stuck out a hand for him to shake. "I'm Lauren Walker. My father is partners with Scott McCallister."

"Oh, yes. Mr. Walker. He's a great guy. I've been looking forward to the start of this gig. It's been a long time since I've had something permanent and at my age, I don't travel so well anymore."

Lauren thought of handing him the employee papers right there, but didn't know if Scott would need to sign them or check them over first. Besides, if she hand-delivered the envelope, she'd have an excuse to see him. *Stop it, Lauren. You shouldn't be thinking about him.*

"I guess I better continue my search," she said. "It was nice meeting you, Hal."

"You, too, Miss Walker. Check the multi-purpose barn over there. I saw Mr. McCallister headed that way while I was unloading my guitars."

"Thanks." Lauren stepped back outside again. "Multi-purpose barn," she muttered. "How many of these old buildings have they fixed up?"

She crossed the dirt walkways to a building she hadn't been in yet. Guests, some she recognized from the cabins, milled about. Some were practicing their roping skills on a fake bull, others sipped lemonade on benches strategically located around the grounds. It made her heart happy to see the dreams of Scott and his parents coming true, even if hers weren't.

At the door to the multi-purpose barn, she heard the sounds of loud music. Not knowing what she might be interrupting, she pushed the door open slowly and peeked around the corner.

The room was nothing more than a large square with folding chairs stacked against the outer walls, leaving the wooden floor free. Two lines of dancers formed across the floor, laughing and cheering as they performed the steps of a country line dance. Lauren remembered Lulu mentioning something about square dance lessons. The scene in front of her must be part of that. She caught sight of Scott watching the dancers from a corner of the room and crossed to him.

"You're a hard man to find this morning," she whispered.

"Sometimes I think it would help to have a clone."

"Are you in here for the entertainment, or to avoid the heat?"

He leaned toward her. "Maybe a little of both."

The music ended and the group clapped.

"I hired a local to teach these classes," he whispered in her ear. "I wanted to make sure the guests were receptive to her."

His warm breath touched her cheek and her heart picked up its pace just from hearing his voice. *Stop it. Now. You can't have him even if you wanted him.*

"Papers," Lauren said, shoving the envelope into his hand and taking a step back. "April sent them."

"You didn't need to bring them all the way up here. I planned to come down."

"It wasn't a problem. I finished cleaning cabins and had nothing else to do." She sighed. "Story of my life right now. I should find some new hobbies."

"Welcome!" a voice called from across the room. "Are you here to dance with us?"

Too late, Lauren realized the woman was talking to her. She turned away from Scott and saw all eyes in the room on her. "I ... uhh—"

"Don't be shy. Come on out here. You'll need a partner for this next dance so bring Mr. McCallister there with you."

Lauren swallowed hard. "I just stopped by to drop something off."

"Good. Now you can stay and dance," the teacher called.

"I've known her for a long time," Scott whispered to Lauren. "She's not going to take no for an answer." He tossed the envelope onto a chair and offered her a hand.

Lauren hesitated before taking it, letting him lead her to the middle of the dance floor. She felt herself blush as they stood under the warm lights and hoped Scott would attribute her red face to the heat from outside.

"My name's Mel. Welcome to our group. We were just about to start the country two-step. You two would make the perfect guinea pigs for this."

"No more line dancing?" Lauren asked weakly. The two-step required physical contact.

"If you want to learn that section, you'll have to come back to tomorrow's class," Mel answered. "Now, Mr. McCallister, take your partner—" She put her hands on her hips. "What's your name?"

"Lauren."

"Beautiful name. Mr. McCallister, take Lauren by the right hand and put your hand right here. Lauren, you put your hand on his shoulder. Right ... here." She lifted Lauren's hand.

Lauren sucked in her breath sharply at the feel of Scott's hand on her waist. They'd touched many times over the years, but never in an intimate way. She couldn't think of a single time when they'd danced together.

"You seem tense," Scott whispered.

"I didn't know I was going to have to dance today," she whispered back. "Once again, I would have worn my boots instead of old tennis shoes. I guess I should just bring them along every day."

"Might be a good idea." He winked.

Mel launched into a series of instructions, walking around the room and adjusting each couple's positions while she talked. She explained the steps of the dance, using Scott and Lauren as examples, and then started the music once more.

"You don't really need lessons, do you?" Scott asked.

She shook her head. "I could dance this in my sleep. Couldn't you?"

"Absolutely."

They danced their way across the wooden floor, dodging couples and Mel as she tried to assist and give pointers to everyone else.

"You know," Scott began, "if we already know how to do this, we can kick it up a notch."

Lauren lifted her eyebrows. "What do you mean?"

"We could add fancy stuff ... like a spin." Without further warning, he let go of her waist and spun her out, still gripping her right hand, then he gently pulled and she twirled back to him.

Back and forth, around and around they danced until the music mercifully stopped. Lauren fell against Scott, breathless and laughing. His arms came around her in a tight hug and she forgot for just a moment that they weren't the only ones in the room as she wrapped her arms around his neck.

"Why didn't we ever do this before?" she asked.

Scott tensed, almost unnoticeably, but Lauren caught the reaction. He let go of her and took a step back. "I should probably take a look at the paperwork you brought."

Lauren frowned. "Is it something I said?"

"No, I just have a lot to do. See ya around."

He left the building without making eye contact. For a brief moment, she'd experienced happiness that she hadn't felt in years—five to be exact. But, Scott's flight from the barn showed once again that her dreams weren't meant to come true.

Chapter 11

With new determination, Lauren left the dance lessons and strode with all the confidence she could muster back to the rental cabins. She left the golf cart at the Double Wind. The time she spent walking would give her time to plan out her thoughts and what she wanted to say to Harris. Her stomach fluttered when she saw him sitting on the stoop to his cabin, a laptop resting on his knees.

"Hey! I was just going to call you," he said.

"You were?"

"I need to know your decision if we're going to get accommodations squared away in time."

Lauren took a deep breath. "This opportunity could be the thing that changes everything for me. Or, it could further mess things up. I know it's a great opportunity that I don't want to miss—"

"But," Harris cut her off. "You're going to pass."

Lauren creased her forehead. "How did you

know?"

"A couple things. First, when you walked toward me just now, you looked nervous. If you planned on coming with me, you would have looked excited and anxious. Second, as much as you want everyone to believe you don't like it here in Midway, I can tell you secretly love it and are happy to be back. And last, you don't want to leave a certain ranch owner."

Lauren's mouth dropped open. "No ... that's not ... no," she sputtered.

Harris laughed at her reaction. "You can't deny it. When McCallister is around, you watch him."

Lauren gasped. "I do not! You make me sound like a stalker."

Harris smiled and reached up for her hand, pulling her down next to him. "I didn't mean it like that. I just noticed that you always know where he is. And, he does the same thing for you. The night we went to dinner, I felt like a third wheel and we never even talked to the guy."

Lauren's face burned. "We were good friends a long time ago. That's all. Besides, he has a girlfriend. She's great and I'd never dream of trying to come between them."

"Why not?" Harris said seriously.

Lauren tilted her head to look at him. "Because it's wrong."

Harris shrugged and returned his attention to the screen of his laptop. "I'm glad we met, Lauren. You made my time here even better than it already was. If I ever make it back to Midway, I'll look you up."

Lauren recognized his words as her dismissal. "You, too. See ya," she mumbled as she stood and walked away. As she'd expected, her presence at the resorts wouldn't make much of a difference to Harris. She wondered how many girls he'd picked up and in how many cities. He was a nice guy, but he'd said it the night before when he made his proposal. He wanted 'no strings attached.'

Back at the farmhouse, Lauren was surprised to see her dad in the kitchen with Lulu. They both leaned over the counter, staring at the newspaper. *Maybe having both of them here will make this easier.*

She cleared her throat and they both turned around. "Hi."

"Hello," her dad said. Lulu nodded.

"I just wanted to apologize for last night."

Lulu shook her head. "We're the ones who need to apologize. You were right. We treated you like a child. It's hard to admit it, but you're not one. Come here." She motioned with her hand.

Lauren approached the counter and Lulu pointed at the paper. It was open to the classified section. They'd circled multiple ads in red.

"Your dad and I were talking and we decided that it's about time I get my own vehicle. With our partnership with the Double Wind and the extra duties that entails, I've been doing a lot more driving back and forth. Having my own car would make a big difference."

"Okay ..." Lauren scooted onto a barstool, wondering what Lulu's announcement could possibly have to do with her.

"We thought if we get one soon, you can use it, too. I know cleaning cabins isn't the job you wanted to come back to. Maybe if you had a car you could try for something in town. You know, until you get back on your feet. You can get your own car and then ... well, you can decide where you want to go from there."

Tears began to build in the corners of Lauren's eyes. "Really? You'd help me like that?"

"We're your parents. It's our job. I know when you first went to Nashville we didn't give you support because we didn't agree with your decision, but even though things didn't work out how you wanted, you never gave up. You just kept pushing forward. That's got to count for something."

"Thank you," Lauren said quietly. "I really appreciate this."

She hugged both her parents. "Anything I can help with in here?" Lauren looked around. "Do you need help finishing bread or anything?"

"Since tomorrow's the 4th of July, and the grand opening, we're not having a dinner tonight," her dad said. "Tomorrow's show is sold out so we'll have eighty people in there."

"There'll be fireworks after and everything," Lulu added.

"Fireworks?" she said with raised brows. "Scott went all out."

"He hopes to make it a yearly holiday tradition."

"Do you plan on going to the parade down in Provo tomorrow?" Lauren asked.

Her dad shook his head. "Not this year. I'd hate to be gone if something comes up. Maybe next year. You're welcome to go."

"Alone? Sounds thrilling. Besides, there's a lot of guests checking out and in tomorrow. I'll need to be at the cabins."

Lulu closed the paper and looked up. "Didn't I tell you? You only need to work Monday through Friday. We have someone else who comes in on the weekends and holidays."

"Oh." *No friends to hang out with and nowhere to go on one of my favorite holidays. I can't wait.*

"Why don't you come up to the Double Wind tomorrow?" her dad said. "We can give you the *official* backstage tour. I'm sure there's things you still haven't seen."

"Maybe," she said noncommittally. "I'll think about it."

Alone in her room, Lauren pondered her situation. With a new vehicle, she'd have a way to get away from the ranch and try to find a job somewhere else. If she was careful and saved everything—not that she had anything or anyone to spend money on—she'd be able to get her own car and apartment sooner than she originally expected.

But something tugged at the back of her mind. *Do I still want to leave? Although I thought I'd hate it here, it's nice to be back. But then there's Scott. I don't want to stick around and be reminded of all the 'what ifs.'*

She stared at her bed and the ugly pink and white comforter. With new determination, she yanked it from her bed and replaced it with one of her brothers' blue and red plaid blankets she found in the linen closet. "It's time to make some changes. Instead of moping around and being a failure. I'm going to go after my dreams again. As soon as I figure out what they are."

Flags hung on each of the cabins the next morning and the barns were draped in red, white, and blue, reminding Lauren of the significance of the day.

"I thought you had the day off today?" April said when Lauren walked through the door of the rental office.

"I do. I just came to get a newspaper. I'm surprised to see you here, too," Lauren answered.

"The other desk clerk asked if I'd work for an hour or two while he goes to the Midway Pioneer Breakfast. He'll be back soon."

"You didn't want to go? You and Scott should have gone over together."

April turned away and looked down at her desk. "Scott's got a lot going on today."

"True. Grand opening day. It's exciting," she said with a grin.

April nodded.

"Will you be there for the opening show tonight?"

April sighed. "I'm not sure yet."

Lauren picked up a newspaper from the stack of free ones by the front door and sat down in a chair. "Are you okay?"

April shook her head. "No. Not really."

Lauren kept the newspaper folded in her lap. "What's wrong?"

"I'm going to break up with Scott," April said quietly.

Lauren gasped. "Oh no! What happened?" She quickly shook her head and put up her hands. "Never mind. It's none of my business."

April came around the desk and sat down next to her. "Actually, it is."

Lauren raised her eyebrows but didn't say anything.

April sighed again. "The moment I heard you were coming back, I knew it was over between the two of us. Scott's been distant ever since you got here. Maybe it's just the stress of opening the Double Wind. I don't know." She paused to take a deep breath. "Anyway, I don't want to stand in your way anymore."

Lauren quickly shook her head. "No, April. That's what *I* don't want to do. I told you before, Scott and I never dated. Ever. We were just friends back then."

"Exactly. Back then. Maybe you two didn't see it, but the rest of us did. Everyone at school knew it was only a matter of time before the two of you were together. I see the way you look at him."

Why does everyone keep saying that? Do I really watch him that much? Has Scott noticed, too? Lauren held up the newspaper. "I came here to get this so I could start looking for job ads. First thing next week I'm going to start turning in applications. When I get enough money, I'll move out and get my own place. I won't be around so much and then I won't be in your way."

April put a hand on Lauren's knee. "It's not that simple."

"Yes, it is," Lauren insisted. "When I left Nashville, I'd just broken up with my boyfriend of four years. It devastated me. I thought we were meant to be together. The night he broke up with me, I thought he was planning to propose."

April lifted her hand and sat back in her chair. "I didn't know. I'm sorry."

"April, he broke up with me because he was

getting back together with his high school girlfriend. It hurt. A lot. I can't do that exact same thing to you and Scott. It wouldn't be fair. Besides, I don't know if he even thinks of me in that way anymore."

"Anymore?" April tilted her head at Lauren. "That one word right there proves my point." She reached over and took both of Lauren's hands in hers. "Scott was never mine to have. He's always been yours. Staying with him wouldn't be fair to any of us. I'm sad because there's a lot of sensitive feelings involved, but not because I'm breaking up with him. It's the right thing to do. He's a great guy, but he's not for me. It wouldn't have worked even if you didn't come back."

The bell above the door jangled as the clerk replacing April walked in. She put a smile on her face and returned to the desk without another word.

Chapter 12

Lauren spent the rest of the morning scouring the newspaper for possible job leads. She ate lunch alone on the back porch of the farmhouse before driving the golf cart over to the show barn at the Double Wind in search of her father. As long as she had nothing better to do, she might as well help him get ready for the evening's festivities. Or, if he didn't need help, she hoped to steal Minnow away for a ride.

"Daddy?" she called as she stepped through the open doors.

"He's not here." Scott's voice was brusque. "He ran to town for a bit."

"Oh."

Scott seemed to be stalking around the room, picking things up and slamming them back down again. She'd never seen him that worked up.

"Is something wrong?" she asked after watching him carefully for a few moments. *Has April talked to him already?*

"What isn't wrong," he mumbled under his breath.

"Anything I can help with?" she asked hesitantly, trying to feel him out.

He turned cold eyes on her. "Let's see. One of the new speakers blew, a food server who was supposed to be working tonight called in sick, our singing cowboy poet went to check out some of the local scenery last night and took a spill. His arm will be in a cast for the rest of the summer which means I don't have a performer for our grand opening. Oh, and did I mention that April just left here? Yeah, she broke up with me. Something about bad timing." He kicked one of the picnic tables. "She got that part right," he muttered.

Lauren stared at him with her mouth hanging open. She forced herself to close it so she could answer. "I'm sorry." *How am I supposed to respond to all that?*

The story of Scott's life falling apart all at once sounded oddly familiar.

"Let me help," she said.

"What can you do? Do you know how to fix sound systems?" he spat.

She took a deep breath. Being rejected by Scott after they were once again on speaking terms would be the ultimate rejection. "Let me work for you. I can help with the show tonight."

He stopped slamming things around and stared at her. "If I hired you, it would only be until our other employee came back."

"I understand that." She twisted her hands together.

"I guess you did get a lot of experience as a

waitress in Nashville." He sighed. "Fine, you can replace our sick food server tonight."

Lauren put her hands on her hips and glared at him. "That's not what I meant and you know it."

"Really, Lauren? What did you mean? You wouldn't possibly expect me to hire someone with your track record as our performer."

"My track record? How could you say that? You used to like listening to me. At least, you claimed to. Some friend you were if you couldn't tell me the truth," she snapped.

"That's not the problem. The problem is that you're a leaver. You left here after we graduated, you left Nashville when things got tough." He paused and lowered his voice. "Your dad told me that reviewer guy who's been staying here invited you to travel with him. You haven't even been back for a week and you're leaving again ... with a stranger."

Lauren gritted her teeth. Scott couldn't possibly know how much his words hurt. She didn't need him to point out the fact that she was a failure. "I turned Harris down. The idea sounded nice, but it ended there. And you *know* why I left here after high school. I had a dream and I followed it. I'm sorry if my leaving was such a problem for you."

"You made yourself heard loud and clear when you left."

"What's that supposed to mean?"

"You turned me down, Lauren. I got it. You didn't feel about me the way I did about you. End of story."

Tears welled up in her eyes. "How dare you! You have no idea how I felt. Leaving you was one of the hardest things I ever did."

"Yet, you made it look so easy."

The tears crested over her eyelids and tumbled down her cheeks but she didn't bother to brush them away. "The night before I left, you came to me and made a grand gesture of professing your love. Of course I loved you back! I think I always did. I'd spent my entire life with a goal of making it to Nashville and you knew it. You waited until the moment I was finally seeing my dreams come true to tell me that you loved me. And then you had the guts to ask me to stay. If you really loved me, you wouldn't have tried to stop me from doing the one thing I'd always wanted to do."

Inside her pocket, Lauren's phone began to ring. The upbeat country song didn't mesh with the mood that had fallen over the barn and she yanked it from her pocket, intent on turning it off. With a quick glance, she looked down at the caller ID. She didn't recognize the number, but knew it was a Nashville area code. *Something is wrong. Is it Ashlyn?*

She brushed the tears away and answered the phone. "Hello?"

"May I speak with Lauren Walker."

"This is she."

"Hi, Lauren. This is Ted Reynolds from Tennessee Boots."

Lauren's heart skipped a beat and a hand flew to her chest. *Why is he calling me?* "Yes, I know who you are." *He's the one who looked the most interested when I performed.*

"Great. You auditioned as a backup singer for us a couple of weeks ago, right?"

"That's correct."

"Well, the person we hired didn't mesh with us

once we started practicing and we mutually decided to part ways. You were next on our list. What do you say? Want to be part of our group?"

Lauren gripped the edge of the nearest picnic table to keep her trembling knees from shaking her to the ground. "Are you serious?"

Ted laughed. "As I'll ever be."

"I'm visiting in Utah right now and I'll need a little time to think about it. Can I call you back?"

"Absolutely. I look forward to hearing from you."

Lauren ended the call and turned back to Scott. His eyes seemed to look right through her. "That was a band I auditioned for in Nashville." Her voice shook. "They want me to join."

"Congratulations. I'm sure when your *visit* to Utah ends, you'll be very happy with your new friends and life." Scott turned on his heel and stalked out of the barn without even a glance her way.

Chapter 13

Lauren gritted her teeth and glared after Scott. *What a jerk. He can't even admit when he's wrong. Is he wrong? Maybe we're both being pigheaded.*

With her head held high and more of her new determination, Lauren stomped out of the barn after him. "Scott!" she yelled.

He kept walking so she had to jog to catch up.

"Give me the keys to your truck," she demanded.

"What?"

"Just do it."

Scott reached into his pocket and reluctantly pulled out his key chain. "What are—"

"I'll be back." Lauren grabbed the keys and ran to the parking area where she knew he left his truck. Driving a vehicle that wasn't twice as old as she was should have made her happy, but that day all she could think about was getting back before Scott made any rash decisions—like cancelling the grand opening.

She skidded to a stop in front of the farmhouse and left the engine running while she ran into the house.

"Lauren?" Lulu called from the kitchen, up to her elbows in bread dough once again.

"Can't talk! I'll explain later!" she yelled as she ran up the stairs. She shuffled through papers she'd brought from Nashville and tossed on her desk the first night home, and then changed from her work clothes into her best audition outfit. She didn't have time to curl her hair, but she didn't need to with her pink cowboy hat on her head. She started to leave, but then turned and grabbed her favorite coral lipstick. "Can't forget this," she whispered.

On the way downstairs, she grabbed her violin case from its spot next to the old upright piano and ran through the screen door. She briefly caught sight of Lulu standing with her mouth hanging open in the middle of the kitchen, but knew she didn't have time to stop.

She drove into the parking lot of the Double Wind at a speed that would have made Scott cringe. Good thing he wasn't outside to see. She waited for the cloud of dust to settle before grabbing her things and jumping out of his truck.

She straightened her hat, lifted her chin, and marched back into the show barn. Scott had returned and so had her father. They both knelt near the stage, messing with what appeared to be a new speaker.

She waited to see if they noticed her, but neither of them looked up. She cleared her throat. Scott glanced up at her and then looked back down, uninterested.

"Excuse me," she called.

Her dad looked up that time. "Hi, honey. Things are a bit crazy around here right now. Did you need something?"

She strode toward the stage. "I'd like to give you my resume." She thrust the paperwork she brought toward Scott. "I understand you are in need of an entertainer and I want to throw my hat in the ring. I'm a two-time Young Utah Fiddling grand champion, I've sung at multiple high-end venues including singing the national anthem at a Utah Jazz game. I lived in Nashville for five years and was able to work with and take classes from some of the nation's top musicians. You can read all about it in the resume. If you'd rather, I can perform for you right now."

Scott's lips stayed in a straight line, but his eyebrows narrowed. Her father looked amused.

Without even looking at the paper in his hand, Scott tried to hand it back to her. "I need someone who will be here at least through the rest of the summer. Sorry."

"I understand that. I live here in Midway now and have no plans to leave."

"What about that band that just called you?"

"I turned them down."

His jaw dropped. "Why would you do something stupid like that?"

Some of her confidence waned when she realized what she was about to say would be witnessed by Scott *and* her father. "Because," she said with a shaky voice. "I'm a person who follows her dreams. I left five years ago to pursue those dreams and I don't regret that choice for a moment, but I left some of my

111

dreams behind when I moved. Dreams change. My dreams now live here in Midway with the Double Wind."

Scott continued to stare at her. She didn't know how to judge his facial expression.

Next to her, her dad cleared his throat. "The entertainment is your department, McCallister. I'll step out, in case you want to conduct an official interview of this applicant."

"Say something," Lauren whispered when Scott continued to stare at her without moving.

"Did you really turn down that band from Nashville?"

"I haven't technically called them yet, but I intend to."

He leaned against one of the tables. "And what if I don't hire you. Would you still call them?"

"Yes. I'm home where I'm supposed to be. I'm with my family, my friends, the mountains I love ..." She forced herself to relax. "Scott, when we were eighteen and you tried to stop me from leaving, I thought you were just saying those things because you were being selfish and didn't want me to leave. It hurt to think that I had such strong feelings for you and you only cared about me when you thought you might lose me."

Scott started to say something, but Lauren put up her hand to stop him. "I don't regret leaving. I learned a lot, had great experiences, and grew up. For five years I tried to convince myself that I wasn't homesick, but now that I'm back, I don't want to leave again. It might mean I'll never be famous for anything, but that's fine. I'm here to stay."

"Are you through?" Scott said with a smile.

"I think so."

"Good. Because I'd like to say something now." He cleared his throat. "You're absolutely right. I told you I loved you because I wanted you to stay. That doesn't mean it wasn't true, but I was convinced that if you left I'd lose you forever. You'd find some city guy with money and fame and completely forget about me." He took his hat off and ran his fingers through his hair. "I wanted to tell you how I felt for years before you left, but never got the courage. I was scared if I told you it would ruin the friendship we already had. When you were gone, I forced myself to go cold turkey. No contact with you. I thought it would be the easiest way. I went to college and immersed myself in my studies. I barely even dated. Then, my parents were suddenly gone. My life became centered around the Double Wind. I thought about you all the time, but never dared think that you'd come back."

Lauren set her violin case on a table and sat down on the bench. "The last five years might have been easier if we'd just called each other once in a while."

Scott sat next to her. "Two stubborn people. Some things never change. I remember going to the movies with you and we watched separate shows because you didn't want to see the one I wanted to watch."

Lauren shook her head. "Your memory fails you. It was *you* that didn't want to see my movie."

"The movie I watched wasn't even any good."

Lauren laughed. "Neither was mine. It was kind of lonely without you there."

Scott stuck out a hand. "Forgive and forget?"

"Forgive and forget." She took his hand and shook it. "Now, about that job …"

Scott threw his head back and laughed. "It's yours. And if I'm being honest, I'm more excited at the thought of you doing shows each night than I was about Hal. The other night, you completely captivated the audience. I've missed the way your music makes me feel."

"Can I make a request?"

"Let me guess. You want a dressing room off the back of the building and you want it filled with bottled spring water and chocolate-dipped strawberries each night."

Lauren grinned. "That sounds great, but my idea is simpler."

Scott raised his eyebrows.

"I want you to perform with me."

"You're kidding."

"I'm not. You and I used to sing together all the time. I can barely play the guitar, but you're not so bad, you know. Just a song or two, that's all I ask. The guests will love seeing the softer side of their riding instructor."

Scott looked down at his hands. "Actually, I've been working on a new tune."

"And?"

"The song you sang the other night, the one about the girl following her dreams? Well, you didn't have any accompaniment with it. The melody stuck with me and I went home and figured out some chords to go with it."

She rested a hand on his arm. "It will be my ending number. I can't wait."

The afternoon passed quickly as Lauren rehearsed. Scott and her dad made sure the new

114

equipment was exactly as it should be. She'd performed many times, but never put on an entire show—especially with only a few hours of prep time. She took notes and wrote scripts and thought of funny anecdotes to share. By the time she felt slightly comfortable with the idea of what she'd be doing, the first guests had arrived.

She'd been so busy, she barely even noticed the servers setting out the food. She vaguely remembered Lulu trying to talk to her and offer her some bread, but she refused, too intent on the task at hand. Finally, with fiddle in hand and a grin that could win awards, she took the stage.

Each song was magnificent. The crowd clapped and cheered and stomped. They laughed at her stories and sang along with the patriotic and folk songs. When Scott took the stage with her at the end of the show, she glowed with happiness. Their voices perfectly paired together as he strummed next to her and sang along on the chorus of her own song. She couldn't imagine a better holiday.

"I'm so happy. I've never felt so alive," she whispered to him behind the curtain they'd set up at the back of the stage.

"I'm glad I got to be a part of it," he said.

"Well, we've always done *everything* together. It's only fitting that you were here for my first real show."

Scott reached out and took her violin from her, carefully setting it down in its case. "There is something we've never done together," he said as he slipped his arms around her waist and pulled her toward him.

Her heart pounded so hard she could barely

breath. "What's that?" she whispered.

"This." He bent down and kissed her. Their lips fit perfectly together and moved together as if they were one.

"We should have done that sooner," Lauren said as they pulled apart.

Outside, pops and bangs signaled the beginning of the firework show. The dinner crowd had exited the building to watch the spectacle. Scott led Lauren to the edge of the stage and they sat down, legs dangling.

She leaned her head on his shoulder as they watched the colors popping in the sky through the open barn doors. "I think all of my dreams just came true."

ABOUT THE AUTHOR

Tifani Clark grew up on a farm in southeastern Idaho (yes, that's where they grow all the potatoes) as the middle of five children. She had a lot of space to imagine and daydream and often pictured herself as a character in one of the many books she read. She was habitually found pretending to be Scarlett O'Hara. She is married to the love of her life and is the mother to four fabulous children. When not writing, she enjoys playing the violin and piano and traveling to new places. She especially enjoys visits to national parks and places of historical significance.